# TAKEN BY SURPRISE

NICOLE J. OWENS

OTHER BOOKS BY NICOLE J. OWENS

*Beneath Your Lies*

# Taken by Surprise

## Nicole J. Owens

Moonlit Graves Publishing

# Trigger Warnings

Thank you so much for picking up *Taken by Surprise*. This little novella started as a scene in my head that I simply could not forget. I knew it would likely never be a full novel, but then I had the idea to try out a novella.

Before you dive into *Taken by Surprise*, as always, I want to take a moment to speak with you. Not just as the author of these pages, but as a fellow human being and a passionate advocate for mental health and emotional well-being.

While this book is lighter and has more humor than *Beneath Your Lies*, it still explores some themes that may be distressing or emotionally triggering for some readers. Though some are not described in heavy detail, I believe it's important to be proactive and share these ahead of time:

— Explicit sexual content

— Criminal activity including human trafficking and breaking & entering

— Alcohol use & abuse

— Emotional heartbreak and relational trauma

If at any point you feel uncomfortable, anxious, or distressed, please know that it's okay to pause, to put the book down, or to step away entirely. Your well-being will always be more important than turning the next page.

You are not alone. You are seen. You are valued.

With endless compassion,

Nicole J. Owens

*To the girlies who don't love Valentine's Day but do love a good dicking down.*

*Cheers to us.*

# Chapter 1

Sipping on my glass of wine, I watch yet another unsuspecting teenager take a pitchfork to the chest.

"Boo," I yell at my TV screen, using the hand not supporting my buzz to hurl a fistful of popcorn at the glowing images. "That's what you get for deciding to hide in the barn."

I sink deeper into my plush, cloud-like sectional. It was originally a soft ivory, and I swore to myself I'd keep it pristine. Spoiler: light-colored couches are not for red wine lovers.

Today is February fourteenth. My least favorite day of the year.

Valentine's Day.

Hence I'm currently curled up on my couch, wine drunk and watching some woefully low budget horror films. It's a tradition. *My* tradition.

The day has always been an annoyance for me. Why do people need an excuse to show their partners they care for them only one day a year? Shouldn't they do that all the other three hundred sixty-four days?

And while we're at it, the mascot is a naked baby with wings.

Am I the only one who finds that incredibly weird?

Warm light spills from the tall floor lamp beside the couch, its brass tripod legs gleaming softly. A black marble coffee table reflects the flickering images from the TV, while the surface is cluttered with my survival essentials: two takeout containers from my favorite local Korean restaurant, an empty bottle of cabernet, the remote, and a bowl of popcorn that has become projectile ammunition for this evening's festivities.

I place the bowl of popcorn back on the coffee table, then grab a takeout container filled with pork katsu before shoveling more into my mouth via chopsticks. The salty crunch is comforting, a small rebellion against the sweetness flooding social media right now. If any romance is happening in this apartment tonight, it would be strictly between me and my pork katsu.

No complaints from me, though.

My phone buzzes on the table, lighting up with a notification. I ignore it. Probably another ad for roses or heart-shaped chocolates. Or worse—another engagement announcement.

Getting engaged on Valentine's Day. How original.

I lean back into my couch cushions, letting the wine settle warmly into my veins. The oversized throw pillows press on either side of me and almost hug me—the only PDA I'll be experiencing tonight. The killer on screen is now stalking his next victim, a girl who clearly skipped the "don't run upstairs" memo. I smirk. Amateur.

I swirl the wine in my glass, watching the deep red cling to the sides like blood. Fitting, considering the carnage on-screen.

Outside, the wind rattles against my windows, a low whistle that makes the shadows in my apartment stretch a little longer. I glance toward the sliding glass door to my balcony. The curtains sway slightly, though I'm sure I locked the door earlier.

Pretty sure.

I take another sip of wine, eyes flicking back to the screen just as the killer raises his weapon. The girl screams, high-pitched and desperate, and for a moment, it sounds like it didn't come from the TV.

Maybe the wine is going to my head, an obvious sign that I should probably slow down on my alcohol intake, but one I actively choose to ignore. Especially today.

I know it's clichéd to have such hatred for Valentine's Day, but I can say that I'm not just some girl who enjoys sucking all the fun out of everything. I'm proud to say I've always disliked this holiday, even as a kid. I often proposed that we didn't need Valentine's Day. In its place, we could have a second Halloween. Surely all the other children would agree with an idea that brought more candy and dressing up. I would dread the day when everyone in class was expected to dole out little cards. Every year I begged my mom to let me do something spooky, but was always shot down. Even now, what could be more on-brand than a bleeding heart?

The year I was in sixth grade, I went against my mom. I used our at-home printer to make my own. I stole images and graphics from some of my favorite horror films, ones my parents likely didn't know I had ever watched. Unfortunately, not everyone was as pleased as I was. My clever trick earned me a prompt trip to the principal's office after the "Scream for Me" Ghostface valentine made Mary Louise sob. She had always been a baby, anyways. My mom grounded me for a month after that, thus ending my reign of Halloween 2.0 over Valentine's Day.

My disdain only worsened after last year's heartbreak, just a few weeks before this terrible day. I knew ghosting was a thing, but who the fuck ghosts someone after six months of seeing each other? I wasn't even that obsessed with Jacob, but rejection hurts, no matter who it's from.

He was attractive, in that approachable way. He had kind eyes that were a soft brown, and his white teeth and inviting smile won me over. He had an athletic build but on the slimmer side. He didn't give the "throw me hard against a wall and fuck me" vibe.

He had recently graduated from MIT and was younger than I typically date, but I was impressed with his courage to approach me at a local dive bar I had gone to with Tiffany. He talked a lot about how he was going to go to law school after he took some time off for himself and how he was going to get a letter of recommendation from the DA.

But then, out of nowhere, the texts completely stopped. We talked at least once every day, no matter how lackluster the conversation was. It made me realize how much I do enjoy having someone to talk to about your day. It broke my heart more than I expected when he just disappeared into thin air.

Maybe he would never have been my future husband and he was a bit too self-obsessed, but he was nice to look at and a good kisser.

Glancing out the window of my twelfth-floor apartment, I let myself wonder for a brief moment what everyone else is doing in the city. A sadness washes over me, and I let myself wallow in it for a minute. Just because I hate Valentine's Day doesn't mean I hate love. I try to bring myself back to the present moment with a reminder that sometimes heartbreak can be good for the soul. Makes you stronger. Harder to break. The things we try to convince ourselves of just before we fall apart.

I go to drain the remnants of what's left in my wine glass, to find it already empty. I peel myself from the couch into standing, to refill my glass, then sneak a peek at the notifications on my phone. One bubble catches my eye. A message from a guy, Shane, I've been casually talking to on a new dating app, appropriately named Pivot. *Designed to change your dating life.*

Blech.

But I assumed it was time to put myself back out there when Jacob didn't resurface.

Shane, a 29-year-old who just moved to the city writes:

***What does a guy have to do to get you to bail on your plans and come out with me tonight?***

I chuckle to myself before typing back a response: ***It would probably require something as serious as taking me hostage.***

Yeah. Like that would ever happen.

# Chapter 2

What Shane doesn't know is that the "hot new spot" I claim to be going to doesn't exist. I do not plan on leaving this couch, but that didn't sound like a sexy thing to relay to my potential new flame.

To be honest, I'm perfectly happy staying at home.

My apartment has always been a safe haven for me. In this city, it's almost impossible to find a one-bedroom apartment that's not the size of a shoebox or costs half of your soul. But somehow, I conjured what little bit of luck I had left and managed to find this place.

I still remember the day I found it.

It was a Tuesday afternoon, the kind that drags its feet and seems utterly pointless. I had been sitting at my desk with my phone, doom-scrolling through listings I couldn't afford and apartments I couldn't stand.

My work laptop was open beside me, a half-finished query timing out on the screen, lines of logic I'd already run a dozen times that day, trying to pinpoint exactly what someone needed. My full-time job is basically making patterns out of messages—cleaning the bad data and finding the story hidden among numbers.

I've always been good at crossword puzzles and finding the differences between two images.

The one benefit to the global pandemic was that my company made its remote-work plan permanent, even when other companies chose to return to the office. While this was great and all, I desperately needed a place of my own. Working from home was not quite the luxury you thought it might be when you had two other roommates.

Just as I was about to give up hope, it appeared: one-bedroom, top floor, "quiet building," suspiciously reasonable rent. No blurry photos. No all-caps warnings. Just a single picture of a sunlit living room with hardwood floors that looked worn in all the right places. I assumed it was a scam. It was too good to be true. I almost scrolled past it.

But something in me paused. Maybe it was fate or maybe it was because I was damn tired of touring places that didn't work out. Maybe it was the tiny note at the bottom that read *available immediately*. I emailed before I could talk myself out of it. Ten minutes later, I got a reply. An hour after that, I was standing outside the building, staring up at the brick building that looked unremarkable in a way that felt safe.

That felt almost like *home*.

Inside, the landlord, Jeff, handed me the keys without hovering, without a sales pitch, like he already knew I'd say yes. The apartment smelled faintly of old books and clean laundry. The windows I've only come to adore more had caught the light of the afternoon sun and softened the noise of the city instead of amplifying it.

Jeff ran a background check, and I signed the lease that same day, heart pounding, afraid that if I hesitated, the universe would snatch it back from me. Ever since, this place has felt like it chose me as much as I chose it.

I've been here for almost two years, and I don't plan to leave any time soon.

It is small but impeccably decorated to my vibes. The half kitchen houses a two-door fridge, a dishwasher (this is absolutely seen as a luxury in a lot of apartments), and enough cabinet space. And another one of the best parts? No roommates. Just me, myself, and I.

What truly won me over about this apartment was the floor-to-ceiling windows, which encase the exteri-

or walls, and give a full view of the city skyline. It is beautiful, especially at night. So many evenings, I spend time just gazing out these windows. My invisibility behind tinted windows makes me feel powerful. Like I'm a watcher of the city.

A wine-drinking Batman, I guess.

Just as I'm settling back down onto the couch with my wine glass filled almost to the brim, I hear an unfamiliar noise outside my apartment door. Probably one of my neighbors coming back to hook up to consummate this rotten holiday.

Lucky for me, my neighbors are mostly quiet and respectful. I haven't really befriended many of them. It's too close proximity for me. The last thing I need is for someone to stop by unannounced, wanting to come hang out inside my apartment. I'm a deeply private person. Blame the Scorpio in me.

No, this is *my* safe space, and it has to remain that way for my sanity.

My phone buzzes again and I look down to see it's Tiffany.

Finally, someone I actually don't mind hearing from on Valentine's Day. I relax a little bit more.

***Just checking on you, girl. I hope you haven't drowned in your self-pity.***

She sends a heart emoji. I roll my eyes and laugh as I type out a response.

***Unfortunately, still chugging along. On my second bottle of wine, though, so no promises.***

The wind outside picks up, rattling the balcony door harder than before. I glance over. The curtains sway like they're breathing on their own.

I used college as my opportunity to get out of the small town I grew up in—Lancaster. I moved to the city for school and was lucky enough to find a full-time job shortly after. My parents had been heartbroken that I would be five hours away, but I liked to remind them that it could always be farther.

The moment I moved into this place, it started to feel like a home. I do miss my parents, but I love the sense of independence that the city gave me. Though I often indulge in my solitude more than most, Tiffany has a lot to do with bringing me out of my shell. I met her the second week I lived here in the laundry room. I was waging war against a washing machine that refused to accept my quarters. She was sitting on the folding table, swinging her legs like she owned the place, bright red lipstick already smeared on the rim of her coffee cup. Without even looking up, she said, "If you kick it just above the coin slot, it works."

It worked. Even though I hadn't felt any doubt, I stared at her like she'd performed a miracle. She grinned, hopped down, and introduced herself. By the time my laundry finished, I knew where she worked, which neighbors to avoid, that her apartment was on the third floor, and that she'd decided we were friends. She helped me carry my warm clothes upstairs and then stayed, sprawled across my living room floor, telling me stories like we'd known each other for years. Like I said, I can be closed off, but Tiffany has definitely broken down some of my walls.

Tiffany is on a date with her girlfriend. Before they met, she would sometimes partake in my annual ritual. Unfortunately for her and for me, Tiffany has always been a hopeless romantic. Valentine's Day is when she comes alive.

Tiffany was bartending when she met her now girlfriend, filling in for a friend on a night she almost skipped. Janelle walked in, soaked from the rain, hair plastered to her face, asking for a whiskey she pronounced wrong. Tiffany corrected her—naturally—then teased her before spilling half the drink down the bar because she couldn't stop staring. Janelle came back the next night to apologize for the whiskey thing.

Then again, the next. Somewhere between last call and closing time, they realized it wasn't just flirting anymore.

Of course, I'm happy for her. All anyone wants for their best friend is to be happy and find someone who deserves them. That's exactly what Janelle is for Tiffany. She's just as deserving of happiness. I couldn't bear to ask what they had planned for this evening, knowing it would probably make my insides turn to Jell-O. But that's the good thing about having a best friend who knows every single piece of you. Tiffany knows better than to gush to me about the extravagant plans she and Janelle probably have for this evening. But even I know that it's my duty, as her best friend, to support her.

***I hope you guys have the most amazing night ever. Tell Janelle I said hi.***

I go to drown more of my sorrow in a takeout container when I hear a soft *tap*. I glance at the screen to find the credits rolling. The sound wasn't from the TV, then.

It was from the glass door leading to my balcony.

I freeze, chopsticks suspended in midair. The curtains shift again, and this time, I see it. It's subtle, but easy to place when you're as familiar with this place as I am. There's no denying its presence—a shadow. Tall. Broad. Growing larger by the second.

My heart kicks against my ribs. I set the container down, every nerve screaming at me to grab my phone, call someone, do something. But before I can move, the lock on the balcony door clicks.

Once. Twice.

The door slides open with a whisper, and I see a shadow growing larger as it steps inside with its back to me.

# Chapter 3

I jump up, grabbing the closest thing that might resemble a weapon. My fingers close around the neck of the wine bottle I recently finished. Not exactly lethal, but it'll do in a pinch. It's the only thing between me and whoever just broke in.

The rush of outside air into my apartment feels cold and intrusive. The air in my apartment feels cold and intrusive. A wave of nausea rolls in my stomach at the realization that I'm no longer safe in my home—this place that has felt like my sanctuary since the day I moved in.

*Survive first. Worry about moving, second.*

I move backward, slow and blind, keeping the wine bottle raised like some kind of trembling sword. The shadows dance around me as I retreat into the darkest corner of the living room, praying that nothing will give away my hiding place.

Heavy footsteps scrape across the hardwood floor.

"I told you I had that," a deep voice growls, low and sharp like gravel. "Fucking show-off."

My breath freezes in my chest.

"Sorry I'm not blessed with your monk-like patience," another voice replies. This one is lighter, dripping with sarcasm. "You were taking forever. Thought you were gonna knit the lock open."

Two.

There are *two* of them.

*I could've taken one,* I lie to myself. *Maybe. Possibly. Okay—maybe not. But two? Hell no. I'm as good as dead.*

I clamp my mouth shut, forcing my breathing to go shallow, quiet. My pulse thunders so loudly, I'm afraid they'll hear it. The bitter metallic taste of fear coats my tongue. With my back against the wall, I slide down into a crouch, doing everything I can to make myself smaller. Invisible.

"Next time," one of them mutters, "can we plan to break into an apartment on the first floor. Or at least someone who has an elevator to their balcony."

A soft thud follows, like he's dropping a bag. "You're the one who said twelve floors was 'nothing,'" the second man says, the once with the deep voice laced with annoyance. "You said—and I quote—'it's basically cardio.'"

"It *was* cardio," the first guy snaps. "I can feel my soul trying to leave my body."

The first guy continues speaking through strained breaths. "Explain to me again, why we didn't just take the stairs like normal criminals?"

"Because," the second guy replies, "normal criminals don't rappel down buildings using a rope they bought at a hardware store five hours ago."

"Cool, cool," the first says. "Just making sure. Because my arms are shaking, and I think I saw God around floor fifteen."

"Floor thirteen," the second one corrects. "He waved."

A pause. "Just give me thirty seconds," the first says. "Then I'll stop sounding like I'm dying."

These two seem to be way too comfortable to have just broken into someone's twelfth-floor apartment. Rappelling down a building? This must be something they do often.

One of them shushes the other. "Why is the TV on? I thought you said no one would be home."

My stomach plummets. This doesn't seem like a random break-in if they were expecting an empty apartment. *My* empty apartment.

"I've been messaging her on that stupid dating app," the sarcastic one says. "Divot or Duvet or some bullshit. She said she had plans and that I'd need to kidnap her to get her to hang out with me. And it's Valentine's Day. Girls are usually out drowning in overpriced cocktails and bad decisions."

Great. Fantastic. I'm being judged for being single while hiding from these criminals. Truly a top-tier moment in my life. But wait—

Messaging me on the app? What the hell?

Shane.

The duo moves deeper into the apartment with slow, confident steps. As they walk farther into the dining room area, I'm able to see them a bit better, though it's too dark to make out many details. I see two large, looming shadows, conveniently dressed in all black. They don't seem hurried in their movements. They walk like they own the place. Like they have all the time in the world.

It takes me a second to notice the fabric masks that adorn their faces.

Concealing your identity can mean only one thing...

They don't plan to leave any witnesses alive.

I sink lower, pressing myself into the wall. I wish I could just disappear. My chest aches from holding my breath. My fingers tremble around the neck of the bottle, my palm slick with sweat.

*Stay small. Stay quiet. Don't die. Preferably.*

What a terrible day to die.

I can see the headlines now: *Miserable Single Girl Dies Brutally on Valentine's Day.*

Some shitty joke about dying from a broken heart or asking if it was a coincidence? If I wasn't about to be murdered, I would probably die from embarrassment right here.

It takes all of my energy to keep myself from crying out.

The intruders' next stop is my kitchen. The sound of one of them rifling through my mail makes my skin crawl. Papers rustle. A drawer opens. Another closes.

In the faint oven light, I'm able to see them a bit more clearly, though any identifiable qualities are still obscured. They're both tall, but one of them stands a few inches higher than the other. Both sets of shoulders are broad and connected to muscular arms straining against black cotton long-sleeved shirts.

The shorter one turns in my direction, and I see dark eyes peering from behind his black mask. Holding my breath, I stare back, unmoving, hopeful that he hasn't noticed me. My eyes well up with unshed tears and my bottom lip quivers.

The staring contest feels never-ending, but he turns his gaze back to the kitchen.

When their footsteps shift direction—back toward the living room—panic slams into me. I slide a hand into my back pocket, only to realize my phone is still on the edge of the coffee table.

"*Fuck*," I mouth, before pressing my lips together. I close my eyes and squeeze them as tightly as I can, silently wishing for them to not come any closer to my hiding spot.

I pause a moment longer with my eyes shut before I hear their footsteps trail away from my location. My eyes pop open and dance around the room to confirm that the coast is clear. No movement. No voices. I take a breath and slowly, I step forward—

And then a gloved hand latches onto my arm from the darkness.

A violent yank tears me off the ground. The wine bottle slips from my grip and thuds onto the rug beneath my feet. Useless. It spins slightly so that the neck points to the figure clutching my arm, like some kind of sadistic game of spin the bottle. The scream tearing through my throat never makes it out as a hand clamps over my mouth, pressing hard enough to leave a mark.

Two black-masked faces stare back at me. One pair of eyes is cold, calculating. Ice blue. The other pair is bright, amused, like this is some kind of game for them. These eyes are the deepest brown I've ever seen.

My heart stops.

"What the hell are you doing here?" Blue Eyes demands, voice like steel.

# Chapter 4
## *Isaac*

What the *fuck* is she doing here? The question detonates in my head the second my hand clamps down over her mouth. She comes apart beneath my grip—pure panic, pure terror. Her body jerks like she's been struck by lightning, and for half a second, my instincts scream at me to tighten my hold, to finish the job before things spiral.

No, that's not the job tonight. It's—

My eyes settle on her face, and everything fractures.

She's not supposed to be here. The apartment was supposed to be empty. Quiet. Clean. In and out. No witnesses. No complications.

I shoot a glare at Zane, my jaw tightening beneath the mask. This is his screwup. His job was to make sure she wouldn't be home tonight. A stupid dating app was his solution.

Clearly, he failed.

This is not the first time we've had a job like this, but it *is* the only time he's fucked up this bad. Part of me wonders if it was intentional. He has been speaking to her for the last few weeks. Could he have developed feelings for her?

There is no way. He'd never put a woman before a mission. No matter how stunning she is.

This is what we do. We don't wear uniforms. We don't do things by the books. No one to call if things go wrong. When a crime is too volatile, too politically inconvenient, or too well insulated to touch through official channels, that's where we come in. Our names are passed quietly from mouth to mouth.

We observe. We intercept. We erase.

Across the street, the building looks ordinary; it is anything but. What functions as a corporate office during the day deals in much darker transactions at night.

At exactly midnight, a transport is scheduled to arrive in the alley behind the building. Unmarked van. False plates. But the cargo isn't drugs or guns.

It's people.

The type of crime that makes my stomach churn. That's what makes this mission so goddamn important. Everything has to be perfect.

We finally have the opportunity to shut this entire ring down.

My hand stays clamped over her mouth, feeling the rapid, shallow breaths she's forcing through her nose. She smells faintly like wine and something sweet—vanilla, maybe. Her eyes are wide, glassy with fear, lashes clumped slightly like she was close to crying before I grabbed her.

Jesus.

She really is beautiful.

Not in the polished, curated way I'm used to noticing with other girls in the city—no perfect lighting, no practiced smile. This is raw. Messy. Her hair's a little wild, her cheeks flushed, lips parted beneath my glove like she might bite me if she gets the chance.

I don't think I'd mind her biting me—

I swallow, hard.

Shit. This is bad. This is very bad.

# Chapter 5

I freeze. My heart pounds so hard it hurts. My chest feels like it could explode. The gloved hand covering my mouth presses a tiny bit tighter.

Brown Eyes tilts his head, eyes crinkling behind the mask. "Well, she's clearly not a ghost, so...surprise?" He shrugs before glancing at the wine bottle now loose on the floor. "Is that your weapon of choice?"

I glare at him. Any reply I try to provide is muffled against the hand still covering my mouth.

"Resourceful," he adds when I don't respond. "I respect it."

"Stop talking," snaps the serious one—Blue Eyes—not even glancing at his partner.

For a moment, I think he's talking to me, but his gloved hand continues to silence me.

"What? I'm saying she's got spirit. And a decent caber-net." He leans closer towards me, lowering his voice like we're sharing a secret. "If you're gonna hit him with that, aim for the temple. It's more effective."

I make a muffled sound that's somewhere between a scream and a curse.

Blue Eyes growls, tightening his grip on my arm. "Enough. We don't have time for this."

"Oh, come on," Brown Eyes says, throwing up his hands. "You're acting like she's a bomb about to go off. She's just—" He pauses, eyes moving to me. "A little drunk, if I had to guess by her glazed eyes. How much have you had to drink, sweetheart?"

Pausing again, I flick my gaze downward toward my mouth to indicate that I'm a bit beyond speaking clearly, in my current predicament.

"She can't answer you with her mouth covered," Blue Eyes says with a huff. "Fucking dumbass." His eyes stay trained on me. "Can I trust you not to scream?"

I shake my head lightly. Now is probably not the time to be honest, but maybe some truthfulness might help me survive the night. The hand presses harder against my mouth. I note how easily he could cover my nose and completely restrict my breathing.

And yet, he doesn't?

*Just get it over with already.*

"A rhetorical question, then," Blue Eyes says. "Listen, we're going to have to do things the hard way until we can trust that you won't freak out on us, okay?" He says it with a sliver of kindness in his voice. "We are not here to hurt you," he adds.

Why do I already feel like I can trust him?

Brown Eyes raises his hands slowly, as if to show me they mean what they say. Blue Eyes doesn't even flinch. He keeps his arm extended to cover my mouth but slowly drops his other hand from my arm. With his now-free hand, he does the unthinkable. He grabs his mask at the back of his neck before pulling it up and off his face.

He has sharp, deliberate features. Cut cheekbones, a strong nose, lips pressed into a line that suggests he doesn't waste words. His blue eyes lock onto mine with unsettling intensity, as if he's cataloging every breath I take. The kind of man who notices everything. The kind of man who makes the decisions. He has curly brown hair that's closely shaved on the sides and a bit disheveled from the mask.

He's—beautiful.

Brown Eyes—still masked—lets out a low whistle. "You're really committing to the dramatic reveal, huh?" He then reaches up and peels his own mask away, dark hair falling messily across his forehead. His grin is slow, easy, and far too charming for someone who just broke into my house. His eyes flick to me, warm and curious, no longer hidden behind his mask. His gaze lingers just a second too long and my pulse stutters. His jet-black hair is longer and straight.

*Focus. Be scared. You* are *scared.*

I can't deny that both of these men are absolutely gorgeous. And they removed their masks—that has to be a good thing.

"Do not scream," Blue Eyes says quietly, before he finally removes his hand from my mouth. It's not a threat. It's a fact. I suck down a deep breath, thankful the barrier is gone.

I swallow hard, still a bit out of breath. "You broke into *my* apartment," I manage, my voice shaking despite my best efforts. "You can't boss me around."

The playful one's gaze drops to the bottle again, then slides back up to my face. "Technically, we let ourselves in. Very different vibes." He tilts his head. "You should really lock your doors."

I shoot him a look sharp enough to cut glass. He must notice the way my body tenses in frustration. His grin widens; he's clearly pleased with himself.

Blue Eyes exhales through his nose, jaw tightening. "You're not helping."

"Oh, I think I am," Brown Eyes counters.

What the fuck is going on?

My heart pounds as I glance between them, cataloging exits, calculating distance. They seem to be more distracted, more interested in bickering with each other. Could I use their broken concentration to my advantage? Could I escape and get away from them? The front door is behind them. No—the hallway is too narrow. If I even tried to run, I wouldn't make it far. They know that. Blue Eyes definitely knows that—his stance subtly shifts, as if he can read my thoughts.

"Are you g—" I try to force the words out before my courage evaporates. Try to say the words that have been ringing in my head since they first stepped into my apartment. "Are you going to kill me?"

They quickly exchange glances. For a moment, neither of them answers. The tension feels heavy in the air as if its about to suffocate me. Then—

Brown Eyes snorts. It's abrupt, loud, and so unexpected that I flinch. I was anticipating a killing blow, not a *snort*.

A second later, Blue Eyes lets out a sharp huff, his shoulders shaking once before he turns his head away,

pressing his fingers to his temple like he's fighting something.

Whatever it is, he loses.

They both burst out laughing.

# Chapter 6

Full, unrestrained laughter fills my living room, echoing off the walls like we aren't standing in the middle of a nightmare scenario.

Brown Eyes bends forward, hands braced on his knees, gasping for air. "Oh—oh God," he manages. "I'm sorry, I'm sorry, it's just—" He doubles over with more laughter before finishing his half-assed apology. "Kill you?" he finishes, wiping at his eyes.

Blue Eyes straightens, still chuckling under his breath, shaking his head. "Absolutely not." Though he's showing only a fraction of joy compared to his counterpart, it's still the most emotion I've seen from him.

I stare at them, stunned. "You're—you're laughing?"

"Because that," Brown Eyes says, pointing at me, "was the most offended I've ever felt in my entire life. And trust me, I was called some pretty heinous things back before I knew how to style my hair properly."

He steps closer before I can stop him, holding his hands up in mock surrender. "What kind of monsters do you think we are?"

"The kind who break into apartments wearing masks?" I shoot back.

Suddenly, their laughter disappears completely. The realization of our situation and my—very warranted—fear settles back in. They are the only ones filled with amusement at this situation. I narrow my eyes at them to emphasize I'm not in on their joke.

"Fair," he concedes easily. "Very fair point."

Blue Eyes' gaze returns to me—steady, sincere, as if the previous few minutes never happened. "We don't hurt civilians," he says. "And we definitely don't kill people for no reason."

I feel a cold sweat break out across my skin, my body trembling as my fear deepens. "No reason?" My voice cracks despite the strength I mustered earlier. 'I'm not sure if you intended for that to make me feel more at ease. And if so, it's not as comforting as you may have thought."

Something like regret flickers across his face. An admission of guilt, of the things he's done. "What I mean is—you're not in danger. Not from us, at least."

Brown Eyes straightens, his grin softer now, less sharp. "If we were here to hurt you, you'd already know it."

My vision blurs slightly, a wave of dizziness crashing over me as my heart races out of control. I choose my next words carefully, a little mad at myself for having the courage to ask. "Do—do you kill people *with* reason?"

Blue Eyes glances at the bottle again on the floor, then at my face, eyes lingering, like he's analyzing the entire situation to determine what answer he will give me. "You're shaking."

I hadn't realized I was, until he noticed. But he's choosing to completely ignore the question. I can't say I'm surprised.

His expression shifts, tension easing just a fraction. "Sit," he says gently, gesturing to the couch where I had been lounging peacefully not too long ago.

Before these two men broke in.

I hesitate.

Brown Eyes tilts his head, dark eyes catching mine, a spark of something unreadable passing between us. "We promise not to laugh again," he says. "At least not *at* you."

My gaze flicks to Blue Eyes, who's watching me close-ly—almost too closely. His eyes seem predatory. His gaze drops to the now useless bottle of wine on the floor, as though he suspects I might lunge for it when given the opportunity, then lift back to my face. Maybe I'll take his partner's advice and smash it right across his temple.

"You don't need that, anyways," he says quietly. "No one here is going to touch you."

The way he says *touch* sends an unwanted shiver down my spine.

I take slow steps toward the couch, which previously felt like a warm cocoon but now more like a prison sentence. As I do, the playful one's smile turns slow and knowing, as if he's noticed my reaction.

"See?" Brown Eyes murmurs. "Trust already."

I don't trust them. Why *should* I trust them?

Without giving myself a chance to overthink the sit-uation, I lunge forward and grab my still very full glass of wine and hurl its contents into the face of the nearest intruder.

# Chapter 7
## Zane

**C**old.

That's my first thought as the wine hits me square in the face, splashing down my face and my neck, soaking straight through my shirt like she's baptized me in bad decisions and worse timing.

I blink once. Twice.

Yep. Definitely wine.

Cheap, too.

I snort, scrubbing a gloved hand down my face as crimson drips from my lashes and runs off my jaw. "Wow," I say mildly. "I can tell by the smell alone—that's not even pretending to be a decent cabernet."

I swipe my thumb across my upper lip and, because I apparently have no self-preservation instinct left, lick it clean.

"Barely any tannins," I add thoughtfully. "Sharp finish. Very bold. Probably on sale."

Beside me, Isaac goes rigid. I can feel the shift in the air—the way his patience snaps taut like a wire pulled too tight.

But me?

I'm...impressed, against my better judgement.

Annoyed, sure. My shirt's ruined, my face is sticky, and this entire situation is spiraling straight into a mess I caused. But still—there's something deeply satisfying about the way she did it. No hesitation. No tears. Just pure, feral defiance.

Yeah. This one has teeth.

I lower my hand and finally look at her properly.

Really look at her.

Her chest is rising fast, eyes blazing, knuckles white where she still grips the empty glass like she's debating whether to throw that, too. There's a wildness to her now that wasn't there seconds ago—fear sharpened into something dangerous.

God.

She's stunning.

And not in the way her dating app photos suggested.

Those pictures? Cute. Pretty. Carefully angled smiles, soft lighting, a little mystery. The kind of beauty you scroll past and then scroll back to because something about it nags at you.

But this?

This is better.

Her cheeks are flushed, lips parted like she's daring one of us to say the wrong thing. Her hair's slightly messy, eyes bright and furious and alive in a way no filtered photo could ever capture. She looks real. Untamed.

More beautiful than she has any right to be.

I exhale slowly, rolling my shoulders as wine continues to drip down my arms. "You know," I say, voice light, almost amused, "I deserved that."

That gets her attention. Her brows knit, confusion flickering through the anger.

"You're more beautiful than your pictures," I say before I can stop myself.

The words hang there, heavy and inappropriate and absolutely the wrong thing to say during a home invasion.

Her breath stutters.

Isaac stiffens beside me.

I know he's going to beat my ass after this. He's all about precision. Getting things done. The type A personality to my type B. He's still pissed off that she's here.

Maybe I didn't do my job as well as I should have, but I can't say I'm upset about her presence.

People's lives are at stake tonight. Our client wants a confirmation. Faces. Timing. Routes.

Because if we're able to give them that information, they can burn the entire pipeline to the ground. Isaac and I have been tracking this ring for months. Clean. Efficient. Military-like precision.

And it's personal for both of us.

I run my fingers through my damp hair before lightly shaking my head to get rid of the droplets of wine. She watches me with such intensity, I almost freeze in place.

I know, with brutal clarity, that I am completely, irrevocably screwed.

Because whatever this job was supposed to be, it stopped being that the second she threw wine in my face and looked at me like she might burn the world down just to survive.

And in that moment, I realized that I'd let her.

# Chapter 8

"So, now will you tell me why you guys are here?" I choke out the words, trying to steady my heartbeat. I drop to my couch, aware that my burst of spontaneity did not help me escape like I hoped.

Brown Eyes' gaze flicks to his partner. A silent exchange passes between them—something practiced, loaded. Then he turns back to me, softer now. Assessing. He doesn't seem as pleased as he was before I threw the wine in his face, but at least he's relatively calm.

"That," he says carefully, "is complicated."

"Try me," I say before quickly wetting my lips. My mouth already feels dry from the wine consumed, and it's as if my adrenaline has made my hangover kick in more quickly.

The serious one studies my face, something un-readable passing through his eyes. Surprise? Approval? "You're calmer than most people would be."

"I'm not calm," I snap. "I'm pretending not to hyper-ventilate."

Something like amusement flashes across his expression before it disappears just as quickly. "Fair."

"I don't know if I'd categorize an attempted drowning as *calm.*"

I can't think straight—my thoughts are darting in every direction, overwhelmed by the sheer weight of panic in this situation. And this motherfucker keeps cracking jokes.

Brown Eyes' hip brushes my shoulder as he walks past me to drop onto the couch with a *thud.* The contact sends an unexpected jolt up my spine. I glare at him, but he only raises an eyebrow, clearly enjoying my reaction.

"You're safe," he says quietly now, the teasing stripped away. "At least, from us." Finally he seems to recognize how terrified I feel in this situation. And how frustrated I am at how they're handling it. "As long as you don't force-feed me any more alcoholic beverages without my permission."

"Shut the fuck up," Blue Eyes demands. "You are safe with us."

My breath catches at the sudden sincerity. I hate that part of me wants to believe him.

Blue Eyes remains standing and I despise that I have to crane my neck to look at him. He glances down at me. I curse myself for how the view causes my thighs to squeeze together. Isn't this what the book girls love?

*Do not think about being on your knees for this man right now, you pervert.*

I can feel his presence like gravity, heavy and inescapable.

"We need something," he says. "And you were...not supposed to be home."

One side of my mouth curls upward in annoyance at his incredibly vague answer. "Obviously."

My eyes dart between them again. The tension in the room coils tighter, thick enough to choke on. Fear hums beneath my skin—but beneath that, something else stirs. Awareness. Curiosity. A traitorous spark of attraction I don't have time to unpack.

Brown Eyes catches me looking at him; his gaze dips briefly to my lips before snapping back to my eyes. A quick, unmistakable side glance. Blue Eyes seems to notice it too—I can tell by the way his jaw tightens, his eyes darkening as they flick to his partner, then back to me.

Dangerous.

Very, very dangerous.

"And if I say no to whatever it is that you need?" I ask.

Blue Eyes holds my gaze, unflinching. "Then tonight gets a lot more difficult."

Brown Eyes straightens, smile gone, tension finally cracking through his easy demeanor. "But," he adds gently, "we'd really prefer not to go that route."

# Chapter 9

I cross my arms over my chest, more for something to do with my trembling hands than any real sense of protection. We all sit in the silence until it stretches so far, I fear it might snap. To be honest, I'm pissed off at myself for wasting that last glass of wine. I wish I had more to settle the nerves pooling in my stomach.

I'm not surprised that I'm the one to break the silence once again.

"You keep saying that you need something from me," I say. "But you're being very vague. If you want me to cooperate, then start talking. And preferably without threats."

Brown Eyes exhales, rolling his shoulders like he's shaking off a persona. "See? This is why I already like her. Despite her...earlier actions."

Both Blue Eyes and I shoot him a look. Clearly, we're both just as annoyed with his jokes and his inability to let things go. "Focus," Blue Eyes tells him.

"I am focused," he replies lightly, before pushing himself closer to me on the couch, giving me his full attention now. No jokes, no grin. The look in his eyes almost takes my breath away. "We're here because there is a trade-off happening tonight."

My stomach tightens. "A...trade-off."

"Yes," the serious one says, his lips set in a flat line. He's already disclosed more than he had wanted to. I can feel how much he wishes I would disappear.

I blink. "I don't understand. What does that have to do with me?"

"This meeting is taking place right across the street," Brown Eyes says as he turns his gaze to my balcony, nodding his head to the building adjacent to mine. "Right over there."

I shake my head. "So, why aren't you over there?"

The playful one tilts his head, studying me. His gaze is sharper now, stripping me bare in a way that makes heat crawl up my neck. "We prefer more of a *surprise* approach. And your apartment," he gestures around before finishing. "It provides the best vantage point."

A cold prickle runs down my spine. I glance past him again, toward the dark glass of my windows. From here, the building across the street looks ordinary. A handful of windows lit. Curtains half-drawn. Nothing that screams *something important is about to happen here.*

I've never even thought twice about that building.

"You broke into my apartment," I say slowly, each word measured, "to watch something happen in another building."

Brown Eyes gives a small shrug. "When you say it like that, it sounds rude."

"It *is* rude," I snap.

Blue Eyes exhales through his nose, the sound tight. "This isn't a sightseeing trip. It's a controlled exchange. Time sensitive. High-risk."

"And you think I'm just going to...what? Make you guys some more popcorn?" I ask. My pulse is thundering in my ears now. "If this is so dangerous, why involve me at all?"

Neither of them answers right away.

Blue Eyes gives Brown Eyes a look of hatred. "You weren't suposed to be involved at all. But clearly that wasn't my job, or else I would've been successful."

Brown Eyes' gaze flicks over to his partner, something unspoken passing between them. It's quick, practiced, a look he's done many times. That alone tells me more than their words ever could.

Blue Eyes finally speaks again. "You're a part of this now, whether we like it or not."

My chest tightens. "That's not an answer."

"It's the only one we can give right now."

I let out a humorless laugh. "You realize how insane this sounds, right? You show up, break into my apartment, threaten me, refuse to explain anything—and expect my cooperation?"

Brown Eyes shifts, finally easing back a step. It's subtle, but intentional. Space. A concession. The movement sends a strange ripple through my chest, like my body notices before my brain does. His shoulders relax just enough to be nonthreatening, his hands staying visible at his sides.

"We're not your enemy," he says, and though his voice is still low, controlled, it softens around the edges. Not gentle. Just...less sharp. Like he's choosing each word carefully now.

I almost laugh again. Almost.

My gaze drifts around the room, and for the first time, I really see it through their point of view. My apartment looks too small with both of them in it—too narrow, too fragile. The couch that once felt safe now seems laughably flimsy. My lamps look like they belong in a dollhouse, their warm light swallowed by the breadth of two men dressed in black. Even the walls feel like they're pressing inward, quietly betraying me.

"Then stop acting like you are," I snap, my voice echoing louder than I expect in the confined space. "I heard you—I wasn't supposed to be home." My pulse thuds in my ears as I gesture vaguely around us. "But sur-fuck-ing-prise—here I am. You don't get to rewind and have a do-over."

Blue Eyes doesn't respond, but I can feel him watching me, assessing. Measuring. Brown Eyes' jaw tightens, like he's biting back something he doesn't want to say yet.

Silence settles again, thick and suffocating, stretching until it feels like it has weight. Each second adds pressure to my lungs. Somewhere outside, a siren cuts through the night—high and distant—before fading away. A car horn blares. Footsteps pass on the sidewalk below.

The city keeps moving. Living. Laughing. Falling in love and breaking hearts. Oblivious to the fact that my world has narrowed down to this room, these two men, and the terrifying certainty that whatever happens next will change everything.

# Chapter 10

My gaze drifts back to my balcony, to the thin line of glass separating my living room from whatever they're waiting for. I feel suddenly exposed—like my walls are made of paper instead of brick.

"And what exactly is my role in this?" I ask quietly.

Blue Eyes finally looks at me directly again. Really looks. My body betrays me by letting out a slight whimper at his intense gaze. "You give us cover," he says. "You let us stay. You don't interfere. And if something goes wrong—"

Brown Eyes cuts in, too quickly, "—it won't."

The interruption is sharp enough that I notice it—the wave of unease that passes so suddenly through this room. I swallow. "You're lying."

Brown Eyes still isn't smiling. "We're *hoping*."

"If we put our trust in you, can we trust you?" Blue Eyes says, voice stern, accusatory.

The room stills. I swallow. My throat feels dry, raw.

Without fully understanding how or why, I nod. Just a small movement. Barely there, but deliberate.

And that realization scares me more than the ask. More than the masks, more than the break-in, more than the fact that two strangers have turned my apartment into a crime scene.

The truth is, I do feel like I can trust them. They haven't harmed me, and they've gone out of their way to convince me.

Blue Eyes tilts his head, studying me. His gaze is sharper now, stripping me bare in a way that makes heat crawl up my neck.

"She's not lying," he murmurs.

Brown Eyes' gaze flick to him. "You sure?"

"Yeah," he says without hesitation. "Heart rate spiked, but not the usual way. We can trust her."

My breath catches and my hands curl tighter around my arms as the weight of everything settles in further around me. "You can tell that just by looking at me?"

His mouth curves, slow and dangerous. "I'm over-observant."

Something about the way he says it makes my pulse stutter anyway, my stomach feeling fluttery. I think about the way he's been overanalyzing me all night, he's barely taken his gaze from me. My cheeks flush at the realization.

The serious man steps closer, close enough that I can smell him—clean, faintly metallic, like rain and steel. He lowers his voice. "You let us do this, and I promise to keep you safe."

"Okay," I say, my voice barely above a whisper. I let my arms fall to my sides, fingers flexing like I'm trying to shake off a numbness that's already sunk too deep. "If something goes wrong," I say carefully, "it comes back to me."

"Yes," Blue Eyes says without hesitation.

Brown Eyes winces. "See, you don't have to say things *that* bluntly."

Blue Eyes leans forward, forearms braced on his knees. His presence is suffocating, but in a good way. He looks steady, immovable—like he's already accepted whatever outcome tonight brings. "That's why we need your consent."

I blink. "My...consent?" My voice rises despite myself. "You're already here. You already chose my apartment.

You already admitted I'm involved whether I want to be or not."

"And we could force the rest," Brown Eyes says quietly. "But that's not how we operate. Plus, we're gentlemen at heart."

Something about the way he says it—too smooth, too rehearsed—sends a chill through me. I lean back into the couch, needing distance from them, desperately searching for more air in my apartment. I turn my head to the side and look out of my balcony. The glass reflects the three of us back: me, pale and tense; Blue Eyes, carved from stone; Brown Eyes, all sharp angles and hidden intentions.

I bite my tongue and hold back a response reminding them that *gentlemen* probably don't break into people's apartments.

"Okay," I say slowly, dragging my gaze back to them. "Then who do you work for?"

Brown Eyes doesn't answer right away. He glances at Blue Eyes—not asking permission but checking alignment. Whatever they are, it's not standard law enforcement. Finally, Blue Eyes speaks, voice still even and infuriatingly calm. "That's not information we can share."

I let out a humorless laugh. "Is there anything you can actually tell me?"

"We told you what you need to know," Brown Eyes says. "Not who signs our paychecks. Not what letterhead they use. Those details don't keep you safe—knowing too much actually does the opposite."

Blue Eyes shifts his weight, just enough to remind me how much space he takes up. "We don't operate through standard police channels. No reports, no uniforms, no paper trail with your name on it. The less you can disclose—willingly or otherwise—the better. Our job is containment. Protection. Discretion. Handling corrupt individuals with untouched power." His eyes lock onto mine. "And right now, discretion includes not answering that question."

I peer down at what I can see of the street. Cars crawl past. A couple laughs as they pass the building entrance across the way. Normal life, unfolding inches from something they don't know about, on a day that's supposed to be all about love.

"So... are people in danger?" I ask.

Their silence tells me the answer they're unwilling to admit. If other people are in danger, then the least I can do is allow these men to use my apartment for surveillance. Who knows how many people would be put into danger if I don't corroborate with them.

I sigh, letting my lungs completely empty of air. "What are we watching across the street?"

Both men go still. I turn my head back just in time to see Blue Eyes' gaze sharpen. "That's also not information we can share." He pauses for a beat. "For your safety."

"Then give me *something*," I say, throwing my hands up in the air in defeat. "Because right now, all I hear is danger and secrecy and 'trust you,' and I don't trust either of you. Can you blame me?"

Brown Eyes studies me, his expression unreadable. "Fair." He reaches into his jeans pocket slowly, deliberately. Every muscle in my body locks.

"Easy, killer," he murmurs. He pulls out a slim device. It's black, rectangular, and blinks once with a soft green light. So, not a weapon. He sets it on the coffee table between us.

"What is that?" I shrink away from it, as if it could explode at any moment.

"Proof," Blue Eyes offers as Brown Eyes taps the device. A voice crackles through the room, one I do not recognize. It sounds a bit distorted, but I'm able to make out a majority of what it's saying, though I can't catch every word.

*"...ten minutes past... no deviations..."*

*"...the building on East Tenth... yeah, the same one..."*

*"...do not be late..."*

My pulse stutters. Another voice overlaps, lower, more cautious. A street name drops. A floor number. Enough landmarks that my stomach tightens as recognition sets in.

My mouth goes dry.

The sound continues, merciless. A further mention of timing. Of a handoff. Of someone being late and how it will *not* be acceptable. Then a soft click as the recording cuts out.

The room feels too small when the silence returns.

My gaze drifts, slow and confused, to my balcony doors and windows. I'm still try to decipher what I just heard.

The space I once adored, now feels tainted. I think of all the times I've stared out those windows or sat on the balcony.

Just what have I been living across the street from?

# Chapter 11

"So, what now?" I ask, shifting once more to try to take up less space on my couch. I guess we're doing this. So much for a quiet night in.

Brown Eyes steps in closer, boxing me in without quite meaning to. Or maybe meaning to very much. His arm brushes mine, deliberately this time, and the air between us hums. "First, we need to trust one another."

"Trust?" I huff a laugh of frustration. "Jesus, we've already established trust. How many times are you going to bring that up?"

He nods in response. "My name is Zane," he adds, placing a hand to his chest. "This is Isaac," he adds as he gestures toward Blue Eyes.

Isaac's eyes cut to Zane in annoyance. They wait for me to reply. My mouth is still dry and for a moment, I think of giving them a fake name. But if they knew they were coming to this apartment, they likely already know who I am. It's probably a test for me.

"I'm Rose."

They nod. A small progression of trust build between three strangers brought together by strange circumstances.

For a moment, I laugh to myself at the realization. "Clever."

Zane eyes me curiously, trying to figure out what I'm referencing. "What is?"

"Shane. Zane. A lot of effort in concealing your identity."

This gets a laugh from Isaac. "He's not very creative."

Zane smiles softly. "Rose on Valentine's Day, huh?" He shakes his head lightly as he laughs a little. "You were using your real name on the dating app."

My spine straightens, a reminder of just how far they've gone to set up everything needed for this evening. I had been talking to "Shane" for at least a few weeks. "At least one of us was."

I feel laid bare in front of these two strangers. I hope I didn't say anything embarrassing to him.

It's as if he can read my thoughts. He chuckles. "Don't worry, Rose, you didn't say or do anything incriminating." His smile softens and his shoulders deflate slightly. "I'm sorry I had to do that to you."

I try to shift the topic of conversation as quickly as possible. "What happens after tonight?" I ask.

Zane's smile fades just a fraction. "That depends on how this ends."

"That's not comforting."

"No," he agrees. "But it's real."

I exhale slowly, then nod toward the balcony. "You said you needed access."

Zane's eyes flick to the glass doors, then back to me. Approval sparks there, quick and unmistakable. "Yes."

"And silence," Isaac adds.

I stand, my knees a little unsteady but my voice firm. "Then we do this my way."

Both of them pause.

"My apartment," I continue. "My rules. You tell me what to watch for. You don't touch anything that isn't yours. And if something goes wrong," I meet Isaac's gaze, then Zane's, "you get me out."

Zane studies me for a long beat. Then he nods once. "Deal."

Isaac, the less agreeable one, hesitates longer. Finally, "Agreed."

I turn toward the balcony doors. The city glows faintly beyond the glass. Somewhere across the street, a clock is ticking down toward a moment that was never supposed to include me.

My awareness sharpens, every nerve lighting up as I stand between them—one steady and intense, the other warm and unpredictable. Their attention presses in from both sides, not just watching me but *feeling* me, a slow, simmering heat that has nothing to do with fear.

I wonder what I've gotten myself into.

"Then," I say, sliding the door open as cold night air spills in, "you'd better at least give me some clue on what we're looking for."

# Chapter 12
## *Isaac*

She negotiates.

That's the first thing I clock once the adrenaline settles.

Not panicked compliance. Not defiance for the sake of it. She lays out terms—clear, measured, delivered with a steadiness that doesn't match the slight tremor in her hands. *My apartment. My rules.* An exit clause. Accountability.

Most people don't think to ask for that.

It makes me reassess her immediately.

Zane agrees too quickly. He always does when he likes someone. I don't miss the way he steps closer, how his arm brushes hers like it's an accident he wouldn't bother denying. I don't miss the hum in the air when she stands between us, either—the way her attention flickers from him to me like she's triangulating something she doesn't yet have words for.

I should shut it down.

I don't.

Because the mission comes first, and she's right—we need the balcony.

I give my agreement last. Not to be difficult, but because once I say yes, there's no version of this night where she isn't involved. Not really. I need to be sure I can live with that.

I can—but that doesn't mean I like it.

When she opens the balcony door, cold air rushes in, carrying the city with it—sirens somewhere distant, the low mechanical breath of traffic, the kind of white noise you forget is dangerous until it isn't.

I step out first. Habit. Positioning. I keep my body angled between Rose and the street, even though she doesn't notice it yet. She's focused on the view—on the building across the way, dark windows stacked like unblinking eyes.

"That one," I say, nodding once.

She follows my line of sight. "The brick building?"

"Yes." Zane joins us at the railing, close enough that I'm aware of him without looking. He leans like this is casual—like we're just neighbors killing time and not tracking a company that might implode the second the truth surfaces. "Fifth floor," he says quietly.

Rose squints. "Looks empty."

"Exactly," I reply.

I pull the compact optic from my jacket, thumb adjusting the focus before I hand it to her. I don't think about how close we are until our fingers brush. She freezes—not startled, not shy. Just registering the contact, the weight of the moment. Then she takes it.

"Empty in the way shell companies are empty," I continue. "The kind of place people pass through."

"And when a transport is coming," Zane adds, "the building comes alive." I can see the discomfort etched on his face.

Rose lifts the optic, posture sharpening instantly. Her breathing evens out, focus snapping into place like this is something she's done before—watching, waiting, piecing things together. I file that observation away, whether I want to or not.

"What are they doing?" she asks.

I swallow hard. It's information I'm not necessarily read to reveal, but like we've discussed, she's a part of this now.

"Staging," I say. "Tonight it's a transfer point. People are brought in, proceed, and moved again before anyone starts asking questions."

Her gaze flicks to me and her eyes widen. "People?"

I hesitate—just long enough to decide how much truth she can handle. This very well be her breaking point in learning how serious this is.

This job is personal for Zane and me. One of the girls who disappeared last year—one of the ones who started the obsession with this job—is a close friend of my little sister. We've been trying to save her and everyone else since we realized her disappearance was connected with this ring.

"Earlier, when the recording mentioned 'cargo', they were talking about human beings." My stomach churns at the admission.

The color drains from Rose's face. Her lips part, but no sound comes out—just a shallow breath that trembles on the way in, like her body has forgotten how to function properly. Her eyes go wide and glassy, fixed on them but not really seeing either man, as if the shape of the truth has finally settled and it's far worse than whatever she'd been imaging.

"Processed how?" Her voice is barely above a whisper. I see her eyes feel with tears at the question.

Rose's apartment offers the only clean sightline. We need this position in order to be successful, and the least we can do is offer her the truth.

"Phones taken," I say carefully. "IDs destroyed. Handlers swapped. Anyone who might recognize them later gets rotated out."

Zane nods his acknowledgement. "They don't stay long. That's the point. Getting tips on locations is far and few, that's why we have to take each one extremely seriously."

Across the street, a single light snaps on—controlled, deliberate. Not a whole office. Just one room.

Zane straightens. "There. That's something."

Rose lowers the optic, pulse quickening. I can see it now—in the tension of her shoulders, the way her jaw sets.

"What does that mean?"

"It means they're prepping the space for the c—" I say. The word "cargo" dies on my tongue when I remember that we're discussing human beings.

"And us?"

I meet her eyes and hold them, making sure she understands the part that matters the most. "It means your apartment gives a clean line of sight into a company that doesn't want to be seen. We have a real chance to stop their organization tonight."

I look at her face and catch the moment it changes. Not all at once, but in layers. The initial horror still lingers in the tight line of her mouth and the way her breath stutters, but beneath it, something harder takes shape. Resolves settles into her posture, straightening her spine. Curiosity flickers behind her eyes, sharp and dangerous, the kind that asks questions even when the answers might cost her. Determination follows, steady and deliberate.

And then there's a brief flicker of something else—a faint spark of adrenaline she hasn't recognized yet, humming just under her skin, quickening her pulse, daring her forward instead of back.

In that instant, I know. She's already made the choice, even if she hasn't said it out loud. She's the kind of person who can't turn away once she understands the stakes. The kind who will put herself in harm's way if it means someone else doesn't have to. Good, to her core—and that goodness is exactly what will pull her into this.

Zane sees it, too. I don't need to look at him to know. The shift is palpable, like a door quietly locking into place. The air between the three of them tightens, charged with something volatile and intimate, something that has very little to do with the criminals we're chasing and everything to do with proximity, with the choices unfolding in real time, with the risk of wanting more than we should.

My focus fractures for half a second too long, tracking the rise and fall of her chest, the way resolve makes her look dangerous in a completely different way. Desire slides in where it doesn't belong, complicating everything, making the stakes feel more person.

The dangerous desire to claim her, pull her into my orbit and keep her there. Consequences be damned. I step back deliberately, breaking the feeling pulsing between us. "Here's what you're about to see," I say, trying to make my voice professional, grounded. "A handoff. It's going to happen tonight. That voice recording confirmed the route and the schedule."

She nods, gripping the optic tighter. "And if something happens?"

I don't soften it; she deserves better than that. She's working with us, and that's much more than we could ask for. "Then we move fast," I say. "And we keep you out of it."

Zane smiles at her—easy, reassuring, dangerously charming. "Trust us, remember?"

She exhales slowly, eyes returning to the building across the street. "I already don't," she says. Then, quieter, more honest, "But I'm here."

That's when it clicks: She isn't just letting us watch from her apartment. She's choosing to stay.

And that choice—brave, reckless, untrained—might be the most volatile variable in this entire operation.

I turn back to face the building across the street, tension aching throughout the muscles in my body.

Because from here on out, exposing these monsters and keeping Rose safe may no longer be two separate objectives. And I know, with a grim kind of clarity, that this—*her*—is going to be a problem I won't be able to outrun.

# Chapter 13

Cold air slices across my scalp as I step back from the railing. The balcony door yawns open behind me, night pouring in—traffic hiss, a siren winding down somewhere distant, the steady pulse of a city that has no idea it's about to be collateral damage.

Inside, my apartment feels smaller. Tighter. Like it's holding its breath with us.

Isaac moves first, crossing the space with quiet efficiency, already checking angles and reflections as if the street might bite if he looks away too long. Zane follows at a slower pace, close enough that his shoulder brushes mine as he passes.

Accidental.

Probably.

The spark between us doesn't care either way.

Across the street, the building no longer looks neutral. Bricks rise out of the darkness, reflective and impersonal, the small number of lit windows deliberate rather than accidental. Three points of light suspended in shadow.

Zane drops into a crouch by the railing and sets his device down, adjusting it with practiced ease. Whatever humor he had earlier is gone. His focus is sharp now, surgical.

"Signal's clean," he murmurs.

Isaac doesn't answer. He's watching the windows like he expects one of them to blink.

I hug my arms tighter around myself, not bothering to hide the shiver. "So this is it," I say quietly. Not a question.

"Yes," Isaac replies. "If it happens, it happens fast."

"How fast?" I ask.

He finally turns to me, blue eyes steady, unflinching. "Minutes."

Zane straightens, the easy looseness draining out of him. "They've been running trafficking routes for years," he says. "Same pattern every time. By the time anyone notices, the damage is already done."

The words land heavier than I expect, sinking into my chest like a stone.

I glance back at the building just as one of the lit windows flickers—once, twice—then steadies again. It's subtle, ordinary. The kind of thing I've probably dismissed hundreds of times.

Zane goes completely still. Isaac's posture tightens beside him, every line of his body snapping into focus.

"There," Zane murmurs. "Handshake."

"What does that mean?" I ask, my pulse ticking faster, skin prickling as the weight of the moment settles in.

"It means someone inside just verified the exchange," Isaac says quietly. "A signal confirming the transfer window—who's in place, who's moving, who's being watched." His gaze stays locked on the building. "It's happening."

The device on the railing emits a soft, almost inaudible tone. Not an alarm—a confirmation.

Zane taps it once. "We're live."

The air changes.

Conversation drops away, replaced by a tension so tight it feels physical. Isaac steps closer to the glass, and without meaning to, I mirror him. Our reflections overlap again—his solid and grounded, mine wound too tight.

"You still okay?" he asks, quieter this time.

The question shouldn't matter. It does.

I nod. "Yeah."

He watches me for a beat longer than necessary, then turns back to the building.

"Then stay where you are," he says. "And tell us if anything changes. Anything."

Zane glances over his shoulder at me. No smile this time—just seriousness. "That includes your gut."

Across the street, one of the remaining lit windows goes dark.

Then another.

My pulse spikes.

Zane inhales sharply. "They're collapsing the floor."

Isaac's jaw tightens. "Transfer's in motion."

The city hum continues below us, oblivious. Cars pass. People laugh. Somewhere, someone is ordering another drink, swiping another card, trusting money they may never see again.

And I'm standing here—between two men I barely know, watching a crime unfold in real time—realizing too late that stepping onto the balcony wasn't the moment I got involved; it was the moment I became part of the fallout.

The last lit window across the street flickers.

Then it holds.

Isaac leans forward. "Here we go."

# Chapter 14

The apartment settles around us, quieter now that the balcony door is closed. Too quiet. Every sound feels amplified—the faint hum of the refrigerator, the whisper of the city through the glass, the soft electronic thrum from the device Isaac has planted near the window.

We fall into an uneasy rhythm.

Isaac stations himself by the window again, posture alert but controlled, like he could hold that position for hours without fatigue. Zane claims the opposite end of the couch, sprawling just enough to look relaxed while his eyes never stop moving. And me—I hover in the middle, unsure where I belong, unsure where I'm safest.

Which is ridiculous, because safety left the building hours ago.

Minutes pass. Then more. Time stretches thin, elastic.

I'm acutely aware of them in ways I don't want to be. The way Isaac shifts his weight when the device emits a soft chirp, his attention sharpening instantly. The way Zane glances at me when he thinks I'm not looking, like he's cataloging reactions instead of objects now. Like I'm another variable he didn't plan for but refuses to ignore.

Zane suddenly stands and drifts in the opposite direction, letting his fingers brush against the back of the couch, the edge of the bookshelf, the counter where one of my abandoned wine bottles still sits. He picks it up and studies the label. "Too bad it's empty, we could've had a glass. Or well, you know, whatever didn't end up on my face."

"I didn't invite you here to judge my wine choice," I remind him. "I didn't invite you here at all."

Isaac turns slightly at that, his attention snapping to us. "Zane."

"What?" Zane raises his hands. "I'm complimenting our civilian."

"More like 'hostage.'" The last word makes the back of my throat taste like bile, realization settling in that that's exactly what I am in this situation. I don't know why I keep acting like an asshole to them. Maybe I'm just beyond confused at this whole situation. I wish I could just keep my mouth shut.

The device hum deepens—barely audible, but Isaac stiffens.

"There," he says quietly.

Zane sits up straighter. "That's the second spike."

My heart kicks hard. "Is that bad?"

"It's expected," Isaac answers. "But the timing's tight."

"Tighter than we like," Zane adds.

I step closer before I realize I'm moving. Isaac notices immediately—not the movement itself, but the proximity. His arm shifts, subtle but deliberate, creating space without pushing me away. A barrier. Or a shield.

I'm not sure which unsettles me more.

Across the street, a light flares briefly, then dims.

Zane exhales through his nose. "They're staging."

"What does that mean?" I ask.

"It means they're nervous," Isaac says. "People get sloppy when they're nervous."

Another chirp from the device, louder this time.

Zane's gaze flicks to me. "You're doing good."

The words land warmer than they should.

"Doing what?" I ask.

"Staying," he says simply.

Isaac doesn't look at me, but his voice softens when he adds, "Most people would've asked us to leave by now."

"I thought about it," I admit. "Briefly."

Zane smiles. "And yet."

"And yet," I echo.

Silence settles again, but it's different now—charged, expectant. Like the air before a storm breaks.

Isaac shifts closer to the window, lowering his voice. "If this goes sideways—"

"I know," I say quickly. "I stay put. I don't interfere."

His head turns, blue eyes pinning me in place. "That's not what I was going to say."

My pulse stutters. "Then what were you going to say?"

"That we leave," he says. "Together."

The word "together" wraps around my ribs, tight and unexpected.

Zane looks between us, something unreadable flashing across his face before he masks it with a grin. "See? Team effort."

Another spike, this one sharp.

Isaac swears under his breath and leans in, fingers flying across the device. Zane's already on his feet, too close now, shoulder nearly brushing mine as he peers at the window.

"Transfer's accelerating," Zane says. "They weren't supposed to push this fast."

"Which means they know something," Isaac replies.

My chest tightens. "About you?"

"About us," Zane says, softer now.

I swallow. The city outside keeps breathing, ignorant and indifferent. Inside my apartment, three heartbeats sync faster, closer, louder.

Isaac straightens abruptly. "Okay."

That single word cuts through everything. "What?" I ask.

He turns to face me fully, expression calm but intent. "We're past observation."

Zane's grin fades. "We're officially part of the night."

I should be afraid.

Instead, standing between them—feeling the gravity of their focus, the heat of their proximity, the way neither of them moves away—I feel something else entirely.

Chosen. Connected. Reckless.

The device emits one long, steady tone.

Isaac reaches out—not touching me, but close enough that I feel the promise of it. "Whatever happens next," he says quietly, "stay with us."

Zane nods. "We've got you."

The city lights flicker across the glass. Somewhere across the street, a decision is being finalized—human beings are being treated like money, lives shifting, consequences locking into place.

# Chapter 15
## Zane

I lean against the doorway, arms crossed, pretending to be casual while my brain is doing somersaults. Rose is in the center of it all—wide-eyed, tense, but not panicked. Not really. And that? That's infuriatingly attractive.

I should be focused. We're on the edge of a major transfer, seconds from chaos. But I can't stop watching her. The way she grips the optic, the tiny bite of her lip, the way she doesn't flinch when Isaac swears under his breath.

She's sharp. Dangerous. And somehow, completely oblivious to the effect she has on me.

I glance at Isaac, who's frozen over the device like it's a bomb ready to detonate. Classic. Blue eyes serious, perfect. And there's me, smirking in the corner like I don't have to do anything important—but also dying a little inside because of Rose.

Great. I've officially become the guy whose entire life revolves around the civilian in the apartment he broke into.

Rose glances over her shoulder, catches me staring. I freeze. She arches an eyebrow. Like she knows. Probably enjoys it. I backpedal with my hands up. "I'm not...I mean, I'm watching...for tactical reasons!"

Yeah, tactical. That's the line. Totally believable.

She shakes her head, goes back to the balcony, and I swear I feel a gravitational pull. I hate that she has this effect on me. I hate it. Love it. Both. Pick one, Zane.

Another chirp from the device. The transfer is moving. Lights flicker across the street. Isaac hisses. I stay leaning, pretending I know what I'm doing, pretending I'm not trying to memorize every detail of her face at the same time.

"She's...remarkable," I murmur to no one, though I know Isaac hears me. He doesn't comment. Typical.

I glance back at Rose again. Yeah, she's trouble. Dangerous, smart, unflinching. And if she survives this night, she'll be the reason I can't sleep for a week. Or a month. Or forever.

I decide not to care. Not yet.

Not until the transfer is done.

Then maybe I can figure out how to tell her she's completely screwed me over—without even touching her.

Mission first. Lustful distraction second. Maybe.

God, she's going to kill me.

# Chapter 16

I try to focus on the building across the street, on the faint hum of the device Zane and Isaac set up, on anything other than the fact that Zane is leaning way too close to me.

It's impossible. My pulse is racing—not just because of the stakeout, not just because we're seconds from a massive transfer, but because of him. Every time I glance at him, something in my chest tightens. I scold myself. I'm not supposed to notice. I'm not supposed to care.

"Focus, Rose," I mutter under my breath.

Isaac is all business, tapping at the device, eyes never leaving the windows. Methodical. Precise. I can almost envy him. Almost.

Zane, on the other hand... he's a walking distraction. He eventually drifts back to the couch, sitting close enough that our knees brush. He doesn't move away. His arm rests along the back of the couch, not touching me—but close.

"You smell good," he murmurs.

I huff a quiet laugh. "Is that part of the operation?"

"Absolutely," he says. "Morale booster. You look too tense."

I bite the inside of my cheek and try to look serious. Pretend I'm a professional. Pretend I'm here to help. But when he smirks at me—one of those slow, teasing smirks—I swear I almost forget what we're doing. I see Isaac glance over his shoulder and catch the way Zane's hand rests just behind me on the cushion. His jaw tightens—then, surprisingly, he doesn't say anything.

Heat coils low in my belly. "Can you blame me?"

Zane offers me a sad smile, softer now. "No, I definitely can't blame you." His eyes look past me and unfocus for just a moment before turning back in my direction. "I'm glad we're here to protect you though. That's the whole reason I've found myself in this..." He twirls his finger in the air as he searches for the right words. "...Unique career path."

The fact that he's offering up pieces of himself to me makes this situation so much more difficult.

He chuckles, that low, amused sound, and I feel it rumble straight through me. I hate it. And yet...I don't.

Minutes stretch, the city humming outside, lights flickering across the street. The device hums softly, registering the transfer in progress. I force my attention back to the task, eyes trained on the building.

"A lot of what I said to you as 'Shane' was true, though—I just wanted you to know that it wasn't all a lie."

"Zane," I whisper. "You said this was just one night."

His eyes meet mine, more serious than I've seen them so far. "It is."

"Then don't make it harder."

He hesitates. Then smiles, soft and a little sad. "Too late."

Inside, I'm begging him to lean forward and press his lips against mine. Emotion swells in my chest—fear, gratitude, something dangerously close to longing. I'm trying to reconcile the man from my phone with the one beside me. Trying not to think about Isaac across the room, steady and watchful. His presence makes me feel...safe.

And yet, I'm so fascinated by both of them. This unconventional job they've found themselves in to protect others. The way they are so adamant about keeping me safe. I feel my chin wobble. And then—

A sound outside. Footsteps. Isaac stiffens, raising a hand.

Everything freezes. The room fills with so much tension and unease that it could very well explode at any moment.

The footsteps pass.

I let out the intake of air I have been holding.

Zane exhales, then looks at me, adrenaline still sharp in his gaze. "You okay?"

I nod, heart racing. "Yeah."

He leans in before I can overthink it again. Like he's reading my mind. It's quick—just a brush of lips against mine, warm and grounding. A kiss that feels like a promise and a goodbye all at once.

When he pulls back, his forehead rests briefly against mine. "For courage," he murmurs.

The night stretches on. And whatever comes next, I know one thing for certain: This was never going to be just surveillance.

# Chapter 17

## *Isaac*

I freeze mid-step, the device in my hands forgotten for a fraction of a second. Of course. Of *course* Zane is leaning in, smirking, and Rose is letting it happen. Letting him get *too close*, letting him touch her. Goddamnit.

My chest tightens, teeth clenching. Part of me wants to storm over there, yank Zane back, remind him what the hell we're supposed to be doing. The mission. The transfer. The fucking company across the street, which could implode at any second.

But another part of me...another part of me doesn't want to move at all. Because the way Rose is looking at him—focused, tense, alive—and the way Zane's smirk softens when he kisses her...I can feel it in my gut. That pull. That ache I've been ignoring.

I step back, letting the shadow of the doorway hide me. My fists unclench. I hate Zane for this, but I hate him even more for being right: Rose is intoxicating. Dangerous. Magnetic. And she's mine, in a way I don't want to admit.

Zane is grinning when they finally pull apart. Relief floods me, and part of me wants to throttle him. Or crawl over and take my turn. God, yes, I *definitely* want a turn.

I swallow, jaw tight. Maybe it's time to stop pretending that keeping her "safe" means keeping my emotions in check. Maybe it's time to stop being the stoic, untouchable one for once. Maybe it's time to *enjoy the chaos*—on my own terms.

The device beeps again, reminding me there's work to be done. The transfer is still happening, moving faster now, lights flickering in sequence. I straighten, tucking the jealousy down behind a mask of professional focus.

But the spark I feel isn't going away. It won't. And when Zane isn't paying attention, I let myself imagine brushing past her, making her laugh, leaning in close...

I clench my jaw, finally smiling to myself. Fine. Let Zane have his fun. I'll bide my time. Watch the pattern, catch the next movement, and then...maybe, just maybe, I'll take my shot.

Because Rose isn't just part of the mission. She's part of me now. And I don't plan on letting her slip away—not for Zane, not for anyone.

The city hums outside, the lights flicker, the device hums softly. The night isn't over.

And neither am I.

# Chapter 18

The kiss lingers long after Zane pulls away. Not just on my lips but in the charged silence that follows. The air feels thicker, heavier, like it's pressing in on us from every direction. Zane stays close, close enough that I can feel the heat of him at my side. His knee is still brushing mine. Neither of us moves it.

Isaac clears his throat, and the sudden interruption startles me. My cheeks redden as I remember we're not alone. And this is supposed to be a job for them.

I look up to find him watching us from across the room, his expression carefully neutral—and failing. His gaze drops, just once, to Zane's mouth. Then to mine. I see something burning behind his eyes that makes me flinch. Is that...jealousy?

Zane is so straight forward, saying exactly what's on his mind, whereas Isaac has me questioning whether he wants to kill me at any given moment. I wish I could tell what he's thinking. He's so cold on the surface, but looks at me with such intensity, I feel like I may melt. But in reality, his friend just kissed me. Clearly, he saw it.

Does Isaac want to kiss me, too? A shiver runs down my spine at the thought of both of them wanting me and I'm flushed with embarrassment at the scenarios that play through my head. The thought of being with both of them. At the same time.

"Positions," Isaac says quietly and I'm, once again, jutted back to the unfortunate reality. This is a stakeout, not a softcore porn.

Zane exhales a slow breath, tension snapping back into place. "Right," he says, keeping his gaze locked on mine. He doesn't move away immediately. Instead, his fingers brush my wrist—light, fleeting, but intentional. A silent *later*.

My pulse spikes and my heartbeat thunders in my ears. My stomach is tied up in knots, and I'm not even sure how we got where we are right now. Valentine's Day has taken a very strange turn.

Isaac returns to the window, but his stance has changed. Tighter. Like he's holding himself in check.

Minutes pass. The city outside glows and flickers. The device on the table hums softly, forgotten but watchful. I try to focus on breathing, on the mundane details of my apartment—the throw pillow, the faint buzz of the fridge—but my body refuses to cooperate. Neither Isaac nor Zane speak. The silence continues to put strain on the situation.

Zane must realize how deep I am inside my own head, and he drifts back towards me again, slower this time. "You're wound tight," he murmurs, the all too familiar cocky smirk spreading across his face.

I huff a laugh. "I wonder why." I gesture around the apartment, like this is a common way to spend an evening.

He smiles, low and dangerous. "We could fix that."

I hate how he has such an effect on me. It's rare to find someone so outspoken and honest. Not to mention he's absolutely breathtaking to look at. I notice just how badly I'm aching for him to kiss me again. Kiss me longer. Deeper. More.

Before I can respond, Isaac speaks without turning around. "Zane."

The other side of the coin: Zane's complete opposite in all ways. Dark, brooding, and hard to read. He is the definition of "tall, dark, and handsome.:

"Too much?" Zane asks lightly, taking one of my hands in his.

*No.*

"Yes."

*Not enough.*

*Not even close.*

"Stop making Rose uncomfortable," Isaac snaps. Annoyance seeps through every single syllable.

I should be grateful for the interruption. Instead, disappointment coils sharp and sudden. Why can't I just tell them how I'm feeling? It's obvious that they feel something too. Zane is clearly pursuing me, but I need Isaac to say something. I can't just disappear with Zane into my bedroom while Isaac stays out here, doing all the work. I wouldn't put it past him to storm into my room, drag Zane from my bed, and kick his ass.

But that's the thing, too. It would almost feel incomplete with just one of them. With them being polar opposites, I want both of them. I bet Isaac is demanding, more dominating. He probably talks girls through it.

A warm heat spreads through my body at the thought of him telling me what a good girl I am.

Zane sinks down onto the floor in front of me instead, leaning back against my knees. The position is casual—intimate in a way that makes my breath hitch. His head tips back, dark eyes meeting mine. Just as easily as I could see what Isaac would be like, images of Zane fill my head completely. He's a giver, and I have no doubt that his partners reap the full benefits of that. He'd probably take his time. Go slow, making sure to pay attention every inch of my body.

"You're doing great," he says again, softer now. "I'm sorry if I'm being too much."

My fingers curl into the fabric of the couch to keep from touching him.

Isaac glances back again. His gaze catches on the sight of us—Zane relaxed between my legs, my knees framing his shoulders—and something flashes across his face. Hunger. Control. Conflict. Even more intense than before.

He steps away from the window, and the room seems to shrink even further.

"I need you to stay focused," Isaac says, but his voice is lower now, rougher around the edges. He stops a few feet from us, towering, his presence commanding attention whether he wants it or not.

"I am focused," Zane replies. "On her."

Every brush of air against my skin feels amplified, my pulse ticking faster like it's counting down. I tell myself to breathe, to think of anything else—but the anticipation of the situation coils tighter, a restless pull I can no longer resist.

Isaac's jaw tightens as he registers the look on my face. His gaze flicks to me, searching. "Is that a problem?"

The question hangs there, dangerous and loaded.

My heart slams against my ribs. "I—" The word catches, useless. I try to finish my sentence, even though my body betrays me, heat crawling under my skin at how closely I'm being watched.

The silence that follows is sharp. Isaac's brow lifts slightly, surprise flickering before something darker settles in its place. For a beat too long, none of us move. In that stillness, the tension hums, alive, waiting for one of us to make a move. Then—

A sharp *ping* cuts through the moment.

All three of us freeze.

The device in Isaac's hand lights up, the glow reflecting off his knuckles—amber first, a warning breath, then red. Numbers cascade down the screen in tight columns, updating faster than my eyes can track, lines blurring into motion rather than meaning. Whatever it says, Isaac understands it instantly.

Isaac is moving before the sound finishes. "There."

The word snaps the room into motion. Zane is already on his feet, every trace of humor and attraction wiped from his face; the force of his departure causes the couch to scrape softly against the floor. "That's not a door alert."

"No," Isaac says, already rotating the screen toward us. "That's internal movement."

My stomach drops, cold and heavy. "Across the street?"

"Yes."

His finger taps the display with surgical precision. One of the previously lit floors blinks out—gone. Another flares brighter, the color deepening, urgent. A third flickers, then stabilizes.

"They're rerouting," Isaac says. "Unscheduled. Too fast."

The heat in the room evaporates, replaced by something cold and razor sharp. I stand, hands trembling. "What does that mean?"

Isaac turns to me, closing the distance in two long strides. "It means something just went wrong."

Zane grabs his jacket, adrenaline sharpening his movements. "Or something just went live."

My chest tightens. "Am I still just...sitting here?"

Isaac's hand comes down on my shoulder—firm, grounding. It feels... possessive. Protective. His thumb presses briefly into my skin, a quiet anchor in the chaos.

"Yes. Lights stay on. TV stays playing. You stay exactly where you are." His voice drops, closer now. "You're doing everything right."

Zane looks at me, expression unreadable for half a second—then softer. "We've got this."

They move back into position, all heat transmuted into focus and urgency. Isaac returns to the window. Zane stations himself near the door—not guarding it, just instinctively placing himself between me and everything else.

I'm left sitting in the middle of my apartment, heart racing, body still humming with everything that almost happened.

Zane flashes me a quick, crooked smile—adrenaline-bright. "Rain check."

Isaac turns to look at me, and I see the hint of a smile at Zane's words. It's small and brief...but it's definitely there.

# Chapter 19

The city doesn't look different after the light goes out across the street. That's the part that unnerves me the most.

No alarms split the night. No shouts from the street below, no flashing sirens or panicked motion. The city keeps breathing the way it always does. Cars sliding through intersections, neon signs hum, windows shine like a constellation that refuses to acknowledge what has changed. One window across the street is dark now, indistinguishable at a glance, swallowed by the glow of everything else.

It is all so subtle. So normal. If Zane and Isaac hadn't broken into my apartment, I'd have no idea that anything nefarious was going on. Me and the rest of the city, probably.

"There," Zane murmurs. "Fourth floor. East side."

Isaac doesn't respond; he doesn't need to. His eyes track the building with a predator's stillness, unblinking, unyielding. One hand braces against the window frame, fingers splayed like he might tear it out if the situation demands it, or launch himself through the glass on instinct alone.

The device hums again, low and insistent. The color shifts—red bleeding into amber, amber cooling into a stark, clinical white.

"That's not right," Zane says, tension threading his voice.

Isaac's fingers move fast across the screen. "They've changed protocols."

My stomach tightens. "Changed how?"

"Not good," Isaac replies. "Means they know something's off."

Across the street, the dark window stays dark. No movement behind it. No lights flicking back on. No correction, no sign of error. Just a void of where something active could be.

The device emits a sudden, piercing tone—sharp enough to cut through the bone.

Isaac's breath goes shallow, his shoulders lifting just a fraction. "That's...not a transfer alert."

Zane leans in, reading over his shoulder. "That's a counter-scan."

My heart slams so hard in my chest that I swear it echoes. "A what?"

"They're sweeping," Zane says grimly. "Looking for eyes."

The air in the room shifts, thick and electric. Isaac straightens slowly, every movement controlled, his gaze darting from the device to the darkened window, then to the walls around us—my walls. "They know they're being watched," he says.

The words hit harder than I expect, knocking the breath from my lungs. "Do they know by who?" I ask.

Isaac doesn't answer right away. His jaw tightens as another line of text scrolls across the screen.

"...Not yet," he says. "But they're narrowing it down."

Zane swears softly under his breath. "That scan radius is tight."

"How tight?" I whisper, afraid to hear the answer.

Zane looks at me—just for a beat—then back at Isaac. "Tight enough that if they triangulate—"

"They could land on this building," Isaac finishes.

Cold floods my veins, sharp and nauseating. My skin prickles, like I've just stepped too close to an open flame.

"You said they didn't know about my apartment." I say, the words coming out smaller than I mean them to.

"They didn't," Isaac replies. "Past tense."

The device pulses again.

This time, the alert is different. Lower, more controlled.

Isaac goes completely still, as if he's listening for something beneath the noise, waiting for the other shoe to drop. Seconds stretch, elastic and unbearable.

"Close call," he says slowly. "They couldn't triangulate our location. We're in the clear."

*For now,* the voice in my head whispers, uninvited and relentless, as I realize just how dangerous this has gotten. I've never felt more vulnerable than I do now. The adrenaline in my body pumps through my veins.

A sudden scraping noise rings out through the apartment—close enough that it feels like it vibrates in the walls themselves.

Isaac moves first, crossing the space in long, silent strides that barely disturb the air. He reaches the hallway light and flicks it off, plunging the living room into gloom broken only by the faint glow of streetlights bleeding in through the windows. The apartment shifts instantly beneath its shadows.

"Stay put," Isaac murmurs to me. He doesn't look back, but the words land with quiet authority, like he knows exactly where I am, exactly what I need.

I nod even though he can't see it, my throat too tight to trust my voice.

The scrape comes again—metal against metal, muted but deliberate. This time there's a quiet click that follows, precise and careful.

Zane's hand lifts, palm out, signaling for me to wait.

Then—footsteps.

Not at the door.

In the hall.

Isaac's head snaps up, sharp and sudden. He checks his device, the faint glow carving hard angles into his face. His jaw tightens. "They're moving past us."

Relief flares in my chest—brief and fragile, like a match struck in wind.

A floorboard creaks somewhere above us.

Zane exhales a curse under his breath, the sound barely audible. "They must have gotten the location of this building and they're checking it," he says. "Trying to flush us out. There is no way they can determine where we are exactly unless we give ourselves away."

A sudden bang cracks through the ceiling—wood slamming hard, a door thrown open upstairs. The sound ricochets down the hall and straight through my nerves. I jump despite myself.

Isaac is beside me instantly, appearing so fast it's almost disorienting. One hand braces on the back of the couch, steady and immovable. The other hovers near my waist, close enough that I can feel the heat of it without the contact. He's not touching me, but he's there, solid, a wall between me and everything else.

"Listen to me," he says quietly, voice low and controlled. "If this goes bad, you go to the bathroom. Lock the door. Get in the tub."

My stomach knots, fear tightening until it aches. "You said I was safe."

His eyes soften for just a second, something human breaking through the steel. "You are," he says. "Because we won't let anything happen to you."

Zane glances back at us then, an unreadable expression flickering across his face at the sight of Isaac so close, so instinctively protective. "Hey," he says lightly, forcing levity where none belongs, though his eyes stay sharp. "When this is over, you still owe me that second kiss."

Heat sparks in my chest—wrong time, wrong place, utterly unavoidable.

I meet his gaze without looking away. "Don't die before you collect."

His smile is quick and bright, adrenaline-lit. "Motivation."

Another sound—closer now. Voices. Low. Male. Too close.

Isaac straightens, every trace of softness gone, his body rigid with intent. "They're on this floor."

# Chapter 20

The moment stretches, thin and electric, like a wire pulled too tight. Then a phone buzzes somewhere in the hall. The voices curse softly, irritation cutting through the tension. Footsteps retreat, fading down the corridor.

Seconds crawl by. Ten. Twenty.

Finally, Isaac exhales, the sound slow and deliberate. "They left."

Zane relaxes just a fraction, rolling his shoulders like he's shaking off the aftermath. "Guess they didn't like their odds."

The adrenaline drains from my system all at once, leaving me shaky, breath unsteady, suddenly acutely aware of where I'm standing—between them again, the danger having stripped away any pretense or distance.

Isaac looks down at me—really looks this time. His hand lifts, hesitates, then cups my elbow, grounding. "You okay?"

I nod, swallowing. "I think so."

Zane steps in close on my other side, mirroring Isaac without meaning to—or maybe exactly meaning to. "You were solid," he says. "Didn't panic. Didn't scream."

"I wanted to," I admit, a breathy confession.

Isaac's thumb brushes my arm, slow and unconscious. Zane notices. His gaze darkens—not jealousy, exactly. Something heavier. More complicated.

The three of us stand there, breath syncing, bodies still humming from the near-miss, the space between us charged with everything unsaid.

The night doesn't settle after that.

It sharpens.

Isaac moves first, returning to the window, but the rigid set of his shoulders tells me he's only half watching the street now. Zane paces the length of the living room once, then twice, like he's burning off adrenaline—or resisting something else entirely.

I stay rooted between them, aware of every breath, every shift of weight. "Whoever that was," I say quietly, "they'll be back."

Isaac shakes his head. "No, they won't."

Zane glances at me. "You're a hell of a deterrent."

I snort softly at the ridiculousness of thinking I deterred anything. "Pretty sure that wasn't me."

His gaze lingers, heated and unapologetic. "Agree to disagree." He steps closer to me, deliberately slow, until his thigh brushes mine. "I feel like we were talking about something important before we were rudely interrupted by some buffoon."

Isaac exhales before stepping in, adjusting the angle of the curtains—his arm lifting just beside my shoulder, his chest close enough that I feel the heat of him. When his hand drops, it doesn't move away.

I'm boxed in again. This time, no danger force it, just straight desire.

Zane's fingers brush my wrist. "You still good?"

My voice comes out quieter than I intend. "I think so."

Isaac's gaze drops to my mouth—just for a second—then back to my eyes. "If this crosses a line—"

"I'll say something," I promise, dizzy with attraction.

The silence that follows is thick, expectant. Zane's thumb traces the inside of my wrist, slow enough to make my pulse jump. Isaac watches it happen, his jaw tightening, not stopping it.

The moment stretches, about to tip into something irreversible. I part my lips, a silent welcoming of whatever decisions we are about to make.

Then Isaac's device vibrates sharply. He pulls it from his pocket, eyes scanning the screen. "They're back at the primary location across the street."

Zane swears softly, stepping back just enough to break the spell while pushing his hands through his hair. "Of course."

The heat doesn't vanish—it just coils tighter, banked and waiting.

Isaac meets my gaze, something intense and unfinished burning there. "We pause," he says.

"For now," Zane adds.

They turn back to the windows, to the night, to the danger circling just out of reach. This untouchable thing that is keeping us apart, fighting against us. But I can't worry about that right now; we have to focus on making sure everyone is safe.

I'm left standing between them, body humming, heart racing, for reasons that have nothing to do with fear.

# Chapter 21
## Zane

Wanting her is the problem.

Not the kind you laugh off or bury under bravado—the kind that slips into your bones and stays there, humming, waiting for you to make a mistake.

I've made a career out of not making those. Or well, besides the mistake about making sure she wasn't home.

But then we wouldn't be in this situation. I wouldn't have met *her.*

Rose sits on the couch, like she hasn't just become the most dangerous variable in my night. Her knees are tucked up, arms wrapped loosely around herself, eyes trained on the darkened building across the street like she can will answers out of the brick walls and windows.

She doesn't look scared enough. Even after everything that's happened tonight: Us breaking in. Explaining what is going on just across the street. Almost being caught by who the fuck knows looking for who is spying on them.

She should be shaking, pacing, demanding explanations. I wouldn't blame her if she was hysterical.

Instead, she's steady.

And, God help me, that makes me want her more.

I lean against the wall near the door, arms crossed, posture casual enough to sell the illusion. That's always been my role—soft edges, easy smile. The one who makes civilians breathe easier while Isaac does the thinking.

Except right now, every breath feels like a risk.

I can still feel her mouth on mine.

Not the kiss itself—brief, controlled—but what it promised. What it nearly turned into. The way her body leaned into me like it recognized something it shouldn't.

I shouldn't have kissed her.

I'd do it again in a heartbeat.

That's the problem.

This mission is delicate. Precision work. Observation, patience, zero footprint. We weren't supposed to *matter*—just be eyes in the dark. Now the dark is looking back, and Rose is standing right in the middle of it.

And I want her.

Not just in the obvious way—though, yeah, that's there, loud and undeniable. I want to touch her, taste her again, feel the way she reacts when I get close. I want to see what she does when she stops holding herself together.

But it's more than that.

I want to protect her in ways this job doesn't allow.

I glance at Isaac across the room. He's at the window again, unreadable as stone, watching, calculating, carrying the weight he always does. He hasn't said it, but I know—he feels it too. The pull. The complication.

Rose isn't just a civilian anymore.

She's a liability. She's leverage.

She's...something else.

The worst part?

She trusts us.

That trust presses against my chest harder than any bullet ever has.

I could cross the room in three steps. She'd let me; I know she would. Her eyes follow me when she thinks I'm not looking. Her body responds before her mind catches up.

I tighten my grip on my own arms, grounding myself.

If we fail tonight, people get hurt—not hypothetically, not eventually but real names. Real faces. The kind that don't fade when you close your eyes.

And if I let myself choose her over the mission?

I'd lose both.

Rose shifts on the couch, glancing my way. Her lips part like she's about to say something—maybe my name. I hope it's my name.

I look away before she can. I need distance. Control. Focus.

So, I stay where I am. I keep watch. And I want her quietly, painfully, in a way I will never let her see—because the mission comes first.

It always does.

Even when it costs me everything.

# Chapter 22
## *Isaac*

I stand at the window long after the city settles back into its rhythm, watching reflections instead of streets—glass layered over glass, my own face ghosted over hers when she moves behind me. The building across the street looks harmless again. Quiet. Normal. That's how it works. Threats don't announce themselves after the fact: They retreat. They regroup. They wait.

So do I.

Behind me, the apartment breathes. Everything is exactly where it should be.

Except me.

I shouldn't still be here. Zane knows it too—but he didn't dare mention it when he grabbed his jacket. His reasoning probably involved giving us space under the excuse of strategy. He's not subtle when he wants to be decent.

Or maybe he saw it before I did. I know he's feeling everything I'm feeling. He's just so much more open about it. He's used to me.

I feel her before I hear her—bare feet against the floor, careful, hesitant. She stops a few feet away, close enough that my awareness sharpens, my body responding before my brain signs off on it.

"You're still watching," she says quietly.

"Yeah." My voice sounds rougher than I intend. "Just making sure nothing else changes."

Silence stretches. Not awkward, but heavy.

"You always do that?" she asks. "Carry the whole room like it's your responsibility?"

I glance at her then. She's wrapped in tension and exhaustion, eyes bright in that way that comes after fear burns off and leaves everything exposed. She looks smaller than she did earlier. Or maybe I'm just seeing her clearer now.

"Someone has to," I say.

Her mouth curves, just a little. "That sounds lonely."

It is. I don't say that.

She steps closer instead, folding herself onto the edge of the couch. She's close enough now that I can feel her warmth even without touching her. My hand tightens against the window frame, knuckles whitening.

I should move away.

I don't.

I turn fully toward her then, giving her my full attention. "You shouldn't be anywhere near all of this. Near us."

"Funny," she replies. "Doesn't feel like you were pushing me away."

I search her face for something—fear, regret, distance. I find none of it, just that same steady pull that's been there since the moment I stepped into her apartment and realized it wasn't just a vantage point—it was a line I *was* going to cross.

"You don't understand what this costs," I say. "What being close to me—"

"I didn't ask for safe," she interrupts. "You asked if I was okay. And I am."

Her leg brushes mine. Accident or not, my body reacts instantly, a low burn igniting beneath my skin. I've spent years training myself out of instinct, out of impulse.

She undoes that in seconds.

Across the room, the city hums. Alive. Indifferent. Outside danger, inside something worse—something I can't outmaneuver or neutralize.

I should step back. Say something measured, professional.

Something in me snaps—not loudly. Quietly. A clean break. I close the distance before I can talk myself out of it, stopping just short of touching her. Close enough that I can feel her breath hitch, see the way her pupils darken.

"This is a bad idea," I say.

She tilts her chin up. "Then stop."

I don't.

I think of protocols. Of consequences. Of Zane and the mission and the thousand reasons I've survived by not doing this.

Then I think of the way she looked when he thought she was in danger—eyes wide, pulse frantic, trusting us with something fragile—and the way she looks now, standing in front of me by choice. Steady. Open. Still here.

My hands find her without hesitation, one bracing at her hip, the other sliding up her back as I press her flush against the cold glass. She gasps softly at the suddenness of it, the sound going straight to my dick. For half a second, I hover there—close enough to feel her breath, to feel the tremor that runs through her body when she realizes what I'm doing.

I give myself one more second of hesitancy, of considering whether this one act will blow up everything I've worked toward. This whole night thrown out the window.

"Fuck it," I mutter, the words barely formed before instinct takes over.

Then, finally, I kiss her.

# Chapter 23

The kiss is not gentle. It's not restrained. It's hours of tension snapping all at once, his mouth claiming mine like the decision had already been made. The window chills my back, and I respond to his lips immediately—hands clutching his jacket, pulling him closer. My body melts into his.

For the first time all night, the noise in my head goes completely quiet.

Our kiss feels like we're both starving. Like we've been denied sustenance for an extremely long period of time. Every glance we shared tonight comes forward in this kiss. His hands move down my body and grip my ass firmly. The feels of his strong hands squeezing me causes a moan to slip from my lips. The noise only sends him deeper into a frenzy.

I don't *ever* want to stop kissing him. This kiss is passionate and sexy. It's everything I fantasized about him. I grind my hips into the crotch of his jeans, and his fingertips squeeze my ass harder before running up my spine to press me deeper into him.

A soft snort of laughter catches me off guard—my own, breathless, tangled up in his lips—just as the front door clicks open behind us.

"Well," Zane's voice drawls from the entryway, too amused for the moment, "that's one way to run over-watch."

I stumble to the side slightly, suddenly aware of how close I'm pressed to Isaac, my hands still clutching his jacket without meaning to. My cheeks burn, and my lips feel full and raw from the kiss. For a moment, neither of us moves.

"You guys started without me?" Zane adds, stepping fully into the room with that signature smirk. "Wow. My heart is broken. Truly. I leave you alone for ten minutes."

I can't help a nervous laugh, trying to disentangle my hands from Isaac's jacket without actually letting go. He doesn't move either. He shouldn't be this close. He shouldn't make me feel like this.

"Perimeter clear," Zane continues, tossing his jacket over a chair like nothing has happened. "Building's quiet. No tails. No surprises." His eyes flick between us, lingering too long on the way Isaac's hand is still at my hip. "Except apparently this."

I flush harder, suddenly aware of the heat rising through me. I clear my throat. "You're impossible," I mutter, mostly at Zane, but I know I'm also talking to the air between Isaac and me.

"You okay?" Zane's tone is soft.

I nod, aware of how my pulse is still hammering in my chest. "Yeah," I manage.

He studies me for a beat, then glances at Isaac. Whatever he's thinking, I can't tell—but the smirk on his face is sharp, knowing. "Huh," he says. "Guess that tension wasn't just tactical."

I glance at Isaac, at the way he's holding himself, the faint brush of his thumb against my arm, and I know he's feeling it, too—just like I am.

Zane lifts his hands in mock surrender. "Relax. I'm kidding. Mostly," he says, then smirks again. "Just...next time, maybe give a guy a heads-up before you shatter the professional atmosphere."

I let out another laugh, easier this time, and my heart still skips when Isaac's gaze lingers on me, quiet and intense. I know, without a doubt, that whatever just happened has changed everything.

And judging by the way Zane looks at us, he knows it, too.

Am I really about to step into this? Am I really about to make this decision?

I extend one hand towards Zane in a silent invitation, keeping my other arm around Isaac. There is no hesitation on Zane's part—he's quick in walking over to me.

"I've been waiting for that second kiss," he says through a smile. He looks briefly at Isaac, who gently nods his approval. I don't know if this is something they've done before, but that doesn't matter. All that matters right now is the three of us. The adrenaline pumping through our veins.

Zane takes my face between his two hands and presses his lips to mine as Isaac leans forward and kisses my neck.

Whatever happens now, I can't blame anyone but myself.

# Chapter 24

I pull my lips from Zane's and turn towards Isaac, shifting right back to the kiss we broke away from when Zane returned. He pulls back and rubs his thumb across my bottom lip, and my eyes flutter.

"I need to know that this is something you actually want," he says, a bit breathless. "That this isn't some fucked-up adrenaline situation."

I bite my lip where his thumb just was, savoring the sensation. "I do want this. I want... both of you." I look between the two of them. "I've wanted it all night."

My admission is all they need. Zane's mouth is on mine within a second and I can feel Isaac press his chest tightly against my back. Zane's hand moves to cradle my head and deepen our kiss, as Isaac drops his lips to the other side of my neck.

*Ooh.*

I moan against Zane's mouth, the feeling of two sets of hands roving over my body almost too much to comprehend. This already feels so good, being cherished by two men at the same time.

Isaac licks from my shoulder to the base of my neck while his hands snake around my waist, his thumbs dipping beneath my sweatpants. My skin responds with goosebumps at his touch. He moves his hands so slowly, trailing from my stomach to my hips to the crease between my thighs. Zane palms my breasts through my shirt as he continues massaging my tongue with his.

I lean back into Isaac, desperate for him to bring his fingers to the one place I'm dying to be touched. Zane's hands slip underneath my T-shirt and roam curiously, before letting my hard nipples peak through the gaps in his fingers. Drawing his fingers closer together, he applies the right amount of pressure to my nipples. I break away from his lips momentarily to take a sharp intake of air.

My mind is swirling. My body is trembling.

I'm so fucking turned on.

"Absolutely perfect," Zane says as he steps forward to kiss me again, pressing his body closer to mine, and I see just how hard he is for me. Isaac finally dips his fingers to where I'm craving friction only to find just how ready I am for both of them.

"Fuck," Isaac groans. "She's already so wet." He slides his finger back and forth, coating his finger in my desire. He presses it deeper to push past my walls and open me up slightly. My knees weaken and I almost think I might hit the floor.

I've been dying to be touched and just the smallest bit of friction has me wondering how quickly I'll come.

*I'm so fucked. Literally and mentally.*

Isaac pulls his hand out of my panties and brings it to my mouth where my lips part, ready to take it into my mouth. "Sorry, princess. First taste is for me," he says before his head leans forward and he pulls his finger to his own mouth.

I gaze up from underneath him, watching his full lips suck his finger clean. He groans with pleasure as he closes his eyes.

"My turn," Zane says as he does the same, flattening his palm against my stomach before sneaking his way into my thong. His body twitches when he hits my sweet spot and sees what Isaac was talking about. How I'm already drenched and they've barely even touched me yet.

Isaac's big hands slip back into the waistline of my pajamas before sliding them down my legs. He moves so slowly that my entire body fills with goosebumps. His rough hands palm my legs as he stands back up. Zane steps back as he grabs the hem of my shirt, tugging the fabric up over my head.

I stand between the two of them in just my panties. I take a step back, then drop down to my knees.

"You don't have—" Isaac starts, but I cut him off by shaking my head.

"I want to," I say, my voice husky. "I want this."

"Well," Zane says as one corner of his mouth tilts up in a smirk. "Show us how much you want us, then."

Isaac's black pants hit the floor and then he's pulling his cock from his briefs before stroking himself slowly. Zane follows suit. I gasp at the sight of both of them. I could feel them just a moment ago, but I hadn't expected both of them to be so big.

I open my mouth, stick out my tongue, and drop my head back. Still stroking his dick, Isaac lightly taps it onto my tongue. "Good girl," he praises as his taps his dick again, a bit harder this time. "Now suck."

I hollow out my cheeks as I try to take him as deeply as I can. I gag around his cock but never break eye contact. Reaching up my left hand, I start stroking Zane's dick. The look of pleasure shining across both of their faces is enough to make me clench my thighs together.

I was afraid I would feel dirty being with two men at the same time. I thought that people would call me a slut if I ever told them what was happening here tonight. But I am feeling the opposite. I am feeling powerful. In control. Like I have both of these men eating out of the palm of my hand.

I want to please them.

Pulling off of Isaac's dick with a pop, I wrap my right hand where my mouth just was and turn toward Zane to put him in my mouth. I bob up and down, watching him take in the sight with his pupils blown. Isaac uses his hand to tighten my grip on his cock while I pump my hand slowly.

We go on like this for a few minutes, letting one slide out of my mouth while I switch to the other. Both of them frequently close their eyes and drop their heads back to stare at the ceiling.

I make it clear how badly I want this. How badly I want *them*. I sit back on my heels and look up at both of them with wide, desperate eyes. "Convincing enough?"

"More than enough," Zane says, breathless, before reaching down to scoop me up. "Now we take care of you." He stands me up so that I'm facing both of them before quickly turning me around and lightly pushing me forward so that my hands fall to the couch.

I look back to see them hungrily gazing at me bent over the couch. They each grab one side of my underwear before tugging them down my legs, leaving me bare and wide open for them. I'm already a soaking disaster and I'm so eager to be touched by both of them. I arch my back a little to poke my ass up further.

"Fucking gorgeous," Isaac says, as he takes in the new view. He drops to his knees, both hands grabbing my hips as he pulls me toward his face and licks up my slit with a flat tongue.

I scream out at the feel of him. The surrealness that he's on his knees for me, licking my pussy like it's the only thing he wants in this world.

"So goddamn sweet," he says before dipping back down to repeat.

My body shudders as he pays extra attention to my clit. "Fuck."

Zane walks around to the back of the couch and grabs my chin with his hand. "If you're going to take us both, we need to make sure you're ready." He lifts my chin to look into his eyes. "We'll make sure you're absolutely drenched and trembling with pleasure before you take our cocks into that sweet pussy."

My walls clench as I listen to what he is saying. Fuck, am I already about to come?

I see Isaac's knees hit the floor as he turns around so that his back is pushed up against the couch. He lifts me by my hips until my knees are bent on the couch and I'm hovering over his face. He makes eye contact with me for just a moment before giving me a wicked smile, and my stomach knots. He's so perfect. They're both perfect.

Pulling me down by my hips, he presses my pussy into his mouth before he lavishes me. A finger disappears inside of me, and I arch my back, desperate for more. He sucks and licks on my clit and I feel my walls clench.

Zane still stands before me, watching as every ounce of pleasure strikes my body. He leans down and kisses me, pressing his tongue into my mouth. "Come on, baby, let it go. Come for him. He wants it so badly."

Just as he says this against my lips, Isaac's tongue intensifies and he sinks another finger into me. I squeal against Zane's mouth at the intrusion, but God, it feels so good. I buck against his mouth and his fingers, wanting more. More.

He knows exactly what I want as his fingers speed up and his tongue sucks on the spot that I need him to pay attention to. I place my hands on the back of the couch to steady myself as I roll my hips over top of his face. Zane stands back and watches me, no doubt anxious for my impending orgasm.

"Y—yes, just like that," I gasp, as my pleasure climbs. "Fuck, I'm—I'm—" Even before I get the words out, an orgasm is tearing through my body and Isaac's tempo does not slow. He keeps ferociously licking me and pressing his fingers into me as he rides out my orgasm with me. Zane watches in delight.

I pant and drop my cheek to the back of the couch. I'm not sure how I'm going to get through the rest of tonight.

I hear Isaac chuckle from behind me. "There's one. How many more can we get from you tonight, princess?"

# Chapter 25

Zane walks behind me on the couch while Isaac comes to stand in front of me.

"I can't wait to see the look on your face while you come," Isaac whispers. His face glistens with remnants of my arousal. He licks his lips as if he's savoring the taste.

"I want—" I rasp, trying to get the words out, but breathless.

I feel Zane wrap his fingers around my hips, holding me in place. He moves one hand to my pussy and slides a finger through my slit. I buck against him with how sensitive I am, but quickly press back against him, eager for him to continue.

"What do you want, princess?" Isaac asks. "Do you want me to fill your mouth?" He palms his throbbing erection.

I nod my head aggressively. I want both of them so badly. I'm eager to please Isaac while Zane fucks me from behind.

I feel Zane's head line up with my center and I try to press back to feel him inside me, but he shifts his cock just out of reach. "Look at our greedy girl," he says, a smirk taking over his mouth. "One dick isn't enough for her."

Isaac takes a step toward me, gripping his cock. He stops just out of my reach, and I crane my neck, trying to reach him with my mouth, while Zane holds my hips in place as he thrusts into me, filling me completely. I cry out from the intrusion.

"How bad do you want it?" Isaac says, toying with me while he pumps his cock with his hand.

"S—so badly," I say. "Please."

Zane is definitely the kinder of the two, whereas Isaac is getting off on this power dynamic. I can't blame him—so am I. "I want you to fuck my face while Zane fucks my pussy."

I chose my words wisely—they send them both into a frenzy. Isaac finally steps close enough for me to take him into my mouth. I start by licking and sucking the head of his cock. Zane pounds into me relentlessly, while simultaneously delivering hard slaps to my ass cheeks.

They sting with the burn, but it feels so good, I don't want him to stop and—

There is a pounding knock on my front door.

# Chapter 26

I gasp, scrambling upright so fast the room tilts. My hand flies to my chest, skin still buzzing, breath shallow and uneven.

The knock comes again, but louder this time. It's clearly not a neighbor's hesitant rap and not a drunken mistake. Three measured hits.

Isaac is around the couch instantly, creating a barrier with his body between me and the front door.

"Don't," he says, low and clipped. His entire demeanor changes. The heat and the softness are completely gone.

Zane's smile is gone, wiped clean like it never existed. He reaches for my wrist, grounding but firm, tightening just enough to tell me that now is a time to be serious.

"Would anyone—anyone at all—have a reason to come here right now?" he asks.

I shake my head, too fast. My stomach twists as I grab the blanket from the couch with shaking hands and wrap it around myself like armor. "I'll just check," I whisper. "The peephole. Just to see—"

"No." Isaac's voice cuts through me like a blade. "That's exactly how they would confirm someone's inside."

My heart slams against my ribcage.

Zane's jaw tightens. He glances at the door, then at Isaac. "If it's someone from the ring," he says quietly, "they won't kick it in right away. They'll wait and listen. They can't afford any mistakes tonight."

The air feels thick, suffocating.

"I heard—" I swallow. "What if it's just a neighbor? We weren't exactly—"

Zane grins. "To what? Remind you of quiet hours?" His smile grows. "I guess they're not used to hearing so much *action* from your apartment, are they?"

I lightly punch his arm, taking offense at his joke but also realizing this man has already seen...a lot of me. Been *inside* me. There is no reason to be shy. They wanted this as much as I did.

"Loud enough to warrant that knock?" Isaac murmurs. "No."

My chest tightens further. His logic is merciless, but accurate.

Slowly, carefully, I edge toward the door anyway, my pulse roaring in my ears. Isaac's hand hovers inches from my shoulder, ready to pull me back.

I rise onto my toes and peer through the peephole. My heart drops—someone has deliberately covered the other side of the peephole so that I can't see who waits for me.

*Oh shit.*

My blood turns to ice.

Just as I go to step back and warn the boys of potential danger, a familiar voice rings out. "Bitch, I know you're in there. I heard...noises."

Relief crashes into me so hard my knees nearly give out.

Tiffany.

Behind me, Isaac doesn't relax and Zane doesn't either.

My nerves settle and I look back to Zane and Isaac to mouth "My friend," and then I place my finger to my lips to tell them to stay quiet.

I unlock the deadbolt and crack open the door. "Hi, Tiff." I force a smile across my features, but I'm sure it's not convincing.

She gives me a strange look before trying to step forward into my apartment. I close the distance another inch but keep my body braced against the door.

"Um?" she asks, waiting for me to get out of the way so that she can come in.

"I thought you were busy with Janelle," I say.

"Yeah, we just got back." Her tone is uncertain. "You haven't answered any of my texts in a few hours, so I wanted to come by and check on you to make sure you hadn't been murdered."

I remain frozen at the door, not letting her in. I hope she can read my eyes and understand that now is not the time for her to barge in like she typically does.

"I'm fine, I promise."

"Okay? And this isn't helping—you acting all weird and refusing to let me inside. That's exactly what someone would do if there was a murderer standing behind them." Her right eyebrow rises.

"Don't be ridiculous," I mutter, trying to conceal my unsteady voice with a laugh. "There's no one here. Just me."

And with what couldn't be worse timing, there comes a crashing sound from behind me in my apartment.

Not a subtle one, either.

Something solid hits the floor with a dull thud, followed by a very male, very unmistakable muttered, "—Shit."

Tiffany's eyes widen. Slowly. Dangerously.

She leans forward, peering over my shoulder like she expects to see a body outline taped to the floor. 'Rose," she says carefully, "tell me right now that you did not just say there is no one in there."

My heart tries to escape through my throat.

"That was—," I start, scrambling, "the cat."

She squints. "You don't have a cat."

"I'm watching a cat," I blurt. "For a friend."

"A cat that swears?"

I open my mouth. Close it. Open it again. I probably look like a fish out of water.

Behind me, the apartment goes dead silent, which somehow makes everything even worse. A poorly concealed secret.

I laugh too loudly. "Wow. You know how old buildings are. Noises. Pipes. Ghosts."

"Ghosts," Tiffany repeats flatly. "Uh-huh. I've lived in this building longer than you. Seen zero ghosts.'

She plants her palm against the door, pushing gently but insistently, and I feel the balance of power shifting in a way I do not like. In a way that I do not need right now. "Move, Rose."

"Please don't come in," I say, a little too fast.

Her gaze sharpens, amusement draining away. "Why?"

Because there are two men in my living room. Because one of them is half-dressed. Because the other one is very naked. Because my Valentine's Day spiraled wildly off script.

Before I can come up with a lie that doesn't sound like a confession, a shadow moves behind me and I freeze.

Tiffany's eyes flick past my shoulder.

Then Zane appears.

He doesn't ease into view or stay discreet like a normal person would. No, of course not: Zane steps right behind me, one arm bracing casually against the wall beside my head, his bare chest very much on display, his grin slow and unapologetic.

"Hey," he says, like this is the most natural thing in the world. "How's it going?"

There is a full three seconds of silence.

Tiffany's mouth opens.

Closes.

Opens again.

Now she looks like the fish.

Her gaze drags from Zane's face to his shoulders to the very obvious lack of clothing and then sneaks back to me. "Rose," she breathes, reverent and horrified all at once, "you said you were staying in. Watching horror movies like every year."

"I am," I hiss, not wanting her to think I've lied to her.

Her lips twitch. "Yeah, well, apparently, you failed to mention that you were having *company* while staying in, watching horror movies."

Zane tilts his head, studying her, offering her that familiar smirk. "She didn't want to be rude."

Tiffany lets out a short, disbelieving laugh. "Oh my God, I leave you for twelve hours and you've already met some hot guy."

"You think I'm hot?" He flutters his eyelashes like he's reveling in the indirect compliment.

"I am begging you to lower your voice," I whisper, trying to push Zane backward with my elbow. He does not budge.

"And—" Tiffany continues, eyes flicking past him into the apartment. "Oh, wow."

My stomach drops. Before I can protest, Zane glances over his shoulder. "Hey, Isaac."

*No.*

*No no no.*

Isaac appears from deeper in the apartment, already dressed but unmistakably present. Zane hooks an arm around his shoulder and drags him closer to the doorway like he's presenting a prize.

"And now I die," I murmur.

Tiffany stares. Actually stares.

Her eyes bounce between the two men, then back to me. Once. Twice. Three times. Then she grins—slow, wicked, and entirely too pleased.

"And your boyfriend has a boyfriend," she says, stepping back into the hallway. "Clearly, I misjudged how your night was going."

I see Zane blink, then look at Isaac thoughtfully. "Wow," he says. "And here I was worried we hadn't defined the relationship yet."

Isaac looks his usual level of uncomfortable and stern. I can't believe Zane is once again making a joke out of a very serious situation.

"Tiff," I warn.

She raises her hands in surrender. "Say no more. I will see myself out."

"Good."

"I'll come by in the morning," she continues brightly. "With coffee. Or maybe hair of the dog." Her gaze flicks pointedly to the men behind me. "And probably some Tylenol. For, you know, post-coitus pain."

"Oh my God," I groan, concealing my face with my palms.

She winks. "Hydrate. Nice to meet your boyfriends who may also be boyfriends."

# Chapter 27

I slam the door shut in her face before she can say anything else. The echo rattles through the apartment like a gunshot, and the lock clicks satisfyingly into place. For a heartbeat, silence hangs heavy, thick enough to almost taste. I lean against the door, chest heaving, trying to calm the sudden adrenaline spike. My heart rate has been like a roller coaster this evening—a continuous stream of highs and lows.

I turn slowly. Both men are standing there, leaning against the wall with those infuriatingly smug, unconcerned facial expressions that makes me want to throttle them.

"That," I say, jabbing my finger straight at them, "was deeply traumatic." My voice cracks slightly, betraying just how shaken I am.

Zane throws back his head and laughs, loud and un-apologetic. "She seems...fun," he says, like he's delivering a compliment and a verdict at the same time.

Isaac clears his throat, but the twitch of his lips betrays his amusement. "You could've warned us," he murmurs, though the corners of his mouth tug upward despite his best effort.

"I tried to," I snap, the words sharper than I intend. "But you—" I gesture wildly, frustrated, "—you made it weird."

Zane arches a brow, the kind of lazy, knowing lift that makes my teeth grind. "Me?"

"Yes. You," I say, squaring my shoulders like I'm ready to defend this accusation in court. "You grabbed him like—like you were introducing a boyfriend."

He shrugs, completely unbothered. "I panicked," he says casually, his voice flat, as if the concept of panic is foreign to him. "The goal was to get her to leave. Mission accomplished."

I press my palms to my face, covering the heat rising up my cheeks. Mortified doesn't even begin to cover it. "I am never opening my door again," I mutter, muffled but deadly serious.

Isaac chuckles softly, a low, warm sound that makes the room feel smaller. "At least she didn't suspect anything else," he says, a hint of pride in his tone.

I can't help it—I glance back at the door, imagining Tiffany's smug little grin peeking through the crack, the way she always looks like she knows exactly what she's doing.

"Oh," I say, my voice dropping to a dark, low growl. "She absolutely did. I'm going to be in big trouble tomorrow."

"I think you're in trouble right now," Zane says. His voice has dropped lower and his eyes are filled with desire again. "The plan was to see how many times you could come, and we only got to one."

They both lean down to kiss each side of my neck. I drop my gaze back and let out a moan. "Is this," I pant before finishing my sentence, though I don't want to make anyone second guess what we're doing—what we're *continuing* to do, "a good idea?"

"It's a very bad idea," Isaac says as he continues licking and grazing my neck with his teeth.

"But shouldn't we—"

*Oh goddamnit, Rose. Just shut up. Don't finish that sentence.*

"—keep an eye on the building?"

Zane pulls back for a second to look into my eyes. "We can stop, if you want to. Our adrenaline was going earlier. We all just kind of lost control. It's really no big deal."

I shake my head furiously. "No, that's the last thing I want. I just—" I pause, trying to decipher between the two conflicting desires in me. "Don't want to be the reason this fails."

Isaac grabs my chin and forces me to look up to him. "This night has been anything but a failure."

Again, his mouth crashes against to mine and I can taste the faintness of me still on his tongue. I let go of the blanket still wrapped around my body and let it hit the floor.

# **Chapter 28**
## *Isaac*

I can feel her pulse thrumming under my fingertips, rapid and alive, and it sends a jolt through me. Her eyes—those sharp, defiant, reckless eyes—are locked on mine, and for another moment, the chaos outside this apartment ceases to exist. It's just her.

Just us.

I press closer, feeling Zane at my side, heat radiating from him in waves that make me clench my jaw. She's caught between us, and a part of me aches to claim her, to make sure she knows that I'm the one she should be listening to—the one she should be trusting in this moment. But even as that thought crosses my mind, I feel that familiar surge of frustration at Zane's boldness. That smug bastard doesn't give a damn about boundaries.

I growl low in my throat, more a warning to Zane than anything else, and tilt her chin just slightly to deepen my kiss. Her lips are soft, warm, and maddeningly yielding. God, she's intoxicating. Every movement, every sigh, every quiver beneath my hands is a reminder that I want more than just this stolen moment—I want all of it.

Her fingers tighten in my hair, and I feel that little hitch in her breath, that hesitation that tells me she's on the edge of losing herself. She wants this, even as she's trying to reason it away, trying to convince herself that it's "a bad idea." But I know better. I *see* better.

"Shh," I murmur against her mouth, just barely audible over the racing of our hearts. My other hand slides down her side, gripping her hip with possessive force. "Tonight is about this."

Zane's presence is constant, the heat and tension between us three like a live wire. I can feel him leaning in, and part of me—one that I hate admitting even to myself—thrills at the thought of her between us.

And then...she steps back to look at both of us. The blanket pools around her feet. God help me, the sight of her bare against the dim light of the room has me seeing red and gold all at once. My hand catches her waist instinctively, pulling her against me, and I feel that little smirk tug at the corner of my lips—the one that's part possessive, part triumphant, and all Isaac.

Because as dangerous at this night is, one thing is painfully clear: I'm not letting her slip away. Not tonight. Not to anything.

Not ever.

# Chapter 29

## *Zane*

♥

Watching Isaac go after her like that—like a predator with all his focus locked on the hunt—is...intoxicating. I've seen that look before, the one that makes him dangerous, magnetic, and nearly impossible to resist. And damn if it doesn't make my pulse spike just as much as hers does.

She shivers under his touch, lets herself melt into him, and I can't deny the rush it gives me. Part of me wants to step in, to claim her right then and there, just to remind him—and her—that I want her too. But there's something delicious in watching him chase what he wants with that single-minded intensity. It's...rare to see him like this.

She looks like she's lost in him, completely oblivious to the fact that I'm here, watching, waiting. And that's fine. Let her. Let Isaac have his moment.

Except, I can't.

She's what I want, too. I've wanted her since the first time she made my blood run hot without even trying. She's reckless, stubborn, infuriating—and every single one of those traits makes me ache in ways I didn't think I could anymore. She's fire, and I'm all too ready to get burned.

So, we'll play this...the three of us. For now. We'll navigate this chaos, figure out the rules later, and enjoy every damn second in the meantime. Sharing isn't ideal. Sharing shouldn't work. But right now, it does, in the maddest, most thrilling way possible.

I take a step closer, letting her scent wash over me. Isaac notices, of course—he's not blind—but I don't back off. Not yet. I want to see him tense, want to see that flicker of possessiveness, because it's real, and it's raw, and it's everything I crave.

And when she finally looks at me—when those wide, heated eyes find mine—I know that whatever this is between us, it's going to be messy. But that's fine. I like chaos.

I *live* for it.

# Chapter 30

I saac presses his hands into my ass cheeks to seamlessly lift me off the floor. My legs snake around his waist; I deepen the kiss. He carries me to my bedroom, Zane's eyes never leave mine. His pupils are blown from desire and his mouth is slightly agape like he can't catch his breath.

My naked body is gently laid across my bed, and I'm enveloped in my warm duvet comforter. At the loss of both of them, I ache, desperate for them to continue covering me with kisses and flicks of their tongues.

They both begin removing what few clothes they managed to put on when Tiffany banged on my door. I prop myself up on my elbows and really watch them this time, since I'm not completely overtaken by lust yet.

They are both all hard lines and chiseled muscles. And still very much ready to continue where we left off, by the looks of it. Isaac moves to my right, as Zane moves to my left.

"Get the fuck over here," I command.

Crawling onto the bed on either side of me, they continue ravaging me like I had hoped. Isaac takes one of my nipples in his mouth as he slides his hand up my thigh. Zane's hand moves to the crease of my thighs before trailing a finger down with my soaked pussy. He grunts his approval before pressing that same finger inside me.

Lightning jolts shoot through my body at the welcomed sensation. It's been barely ten minutes since I had him inside me, and it feels like centuries. I'm absolutely craving his touch, the intense ride up before my orgasm comes crashing down.

Isaac drops feather-light kisses up my body until his mouth is pressed against mine again. "What do you want, princess?" he says against my mouth before looking out of the side of his eye to see Zane's hand working my pussy.

"I want—" Words are too difficult right now. Not when I can taste myself on Isaac's tongue and Zane adds another finger before pulsing them in and out at a steady rhythm. "I—"

Zane lets out a small laugh and looks up at me, bright white teeth on full display. "You've gotta use those words, baby." He adds a third finger, and my hips buck off the bed.

Isaac pulls his lips from mine and slides his palm down my body until he reaches my clit and begins rubbing it.

"Shit—" Now I officially have mush for brains. Fuck, I'm going to come again just from this.

"That's it, come for us, baby," Zane says, speeding up his fingers and curling them so they hit the exact spot I need to be pushed over the edge. "Come all over my hand and then tell us what you want."

My back bows off the bed and in unison, both of them begin licking and sucking on my nipples. My orgasm tears through me and my body quivers as the three of us ride it out, them never stopping their hands or their mouths.

"Fuck—" I pant as I drop my head back to the bed.

Grabbing my chin with the hand he just used to get me off, Zane presses his lips into mine and kisses me ferociously, like he's trying to swallow me. Isaac moves his fingers from my clit further down my slit. At a slow pace, he caresses me up and down, further slickening every inch of me.

The wave of another orgasm has me feeling positively warm and like I'm floating. Words are no longer difficult, and I'm beyond ready to tell them exactly what I want from them.

"I want—" I suck in a sharp intake of breath as Zane adjusts himself so that he is perpendicular to my body. He slides down between my legs to patiently wait for me to finish my request.

He beams up at me like he's very aware of the effect he has on me while lying between my legs, just inches from the cunt he's already fucked with his fingers and his dick. Subconsciously, my body shifts slightly down to try to close the gap between us, eager to feel his mouth where his fingers just were.

"You were saying?" Isaac asks, his hand now gripping my hip with intensity.

"I want both of you." I manage to force the words out, not feeling as guilty or judged as I thought I would.

Zane cocks an eyebrow at me, not fully understanding my meaning.

"I mean, I want both of you to fuck me at the same time."

Zane's eyes widen in surprise and sheer glee. "You want one of us here?" he asks, as he presses a finger to my asshole.

I can't help but clench at the feeling, but I nod my head in response. "Yes, that's exactly what I want."

He moves his finger back to the dampness between my legs and coats it in my cum before pressing it back down. "We can absolutely do that for you, baby. But you need to relax." Only a second passes between him finishing his sentence and his mouth dropping down to my pussy. He licks and sucks on my clit as he works just the tip of his finger into my ass.

My whole body clenches and I know it won't be long before I'm coming again. I lie back to stare at the ceiling, then turn my head to see the most genuine smile on Isaac's face. It surprises me almost as much as anything else this evening.

"You are so beautiful," he says lightly, brushing a strand of hair off my forehead. He leans forward and gives me another kiss that makes me forget everything else entirely. Except for his friend between my legs, expertly licking my pussy and getting my asshole ready to take him.

Zane backs off just for a moment while Isaac rolls me on top of him. This position is so intimate, I feel like I could stare into his eyes forever. I grind my hips into his stomach, feeling my slickness rub off on him.

"Holy fuck," he hisses. "You're so wet." He grips my hips with his hands and moves with me as I grind on top of him. It's just enough friction that I could get off, but I'm afraid we're getting into territory where I might tire out. I reach down between us and grip his cock in my fist, lining it up perfectly with my entrance. I slide down it tantalizingly slow. The slight burn as my body stretches around him to take him deeper has me moaning. He reaches between us and rubs his thumb on my clit.

"Yeah, just like that," he says between grunts.

I feel Zane biting and kissing my ass cheeks, giving them an occasional slap that makes my head jerk back. "Fuck my ass, Zane. I have lube in my nightstand."

He flies off the bed over my wooden nightstand; he flings open the drawer and secures what he needs. He moves back behind me again and Isaac slows his rhythm.

The lube is warmer than I expected as it drips down my ass crack.

Scooping some up, Zane slowly presses his lubricated finger into my asshole before twirling it around. "Baby, relax. It's already going to be a tight fit with both of us."

I close my eyes and sink down onto Isaac's cock and Zane's finger. Moving at a very slow pace, I keep this up as Zane works to get me ready. I glance down at Isaac and see that his eyes are still trained on me. He's not moving;

he's watching me very cautiously. Letting me make all the moves now.

"Feel good?" Isaac asks.

I subtly nod my head, feeling delirious with my building orgasm. "Yeah."

I feel the bed shift as Zane moves behind me. He lines his cock up at my entrance before pressing the head in. It burns and I almost jump off the bed. The feeling of both of their cocks inside of me is more than I imagined. I lift up and tilt forward to bury my face in Isaac's neck.

"You tell us if it's too much," he says into my hair before planting a kiss on my temple.

I nod my head to let him know I heard him. 'I don't want to stop."

"Take what you want from us, baby girl," Zane says. "We're all yours."

I shift my hips down and back, taking Isaac back into my pussy and pressing further down on Zane's dick. I feel like I'm on fire, my body being stretched in a way that hurts, but also feels so fucking good. I lift my hips up before repeating the action, waiting until my ass is comfortable enough to take more of Zane.

Isaac's hands bite in my hip bones and Zane grips my ass.

"Fuck, look at how she takes us both so well," Zane says, delivering a swift slap to my ass. "This is a fucking beautiful sight."

I speed up my space, the burn now subsiding and only pleasure seeping through. Isaac moves his hand back to circling my clit as I tilt my head up to try to get a breath. He takes my nipple in his mouth and lightly grazes his teeth on it before biting down.

Jesus, fuck. I'm not going to last much longer.

"Harder," I snap at anyone. At everyone. Knowing my orgasm is building and it's going to tear me apart when it comes. I've never experienced this much pleasure at once—the feel of Zane burying his cock into my ass, squeezing my cheeks, and Isaac biting my nipple, massaging my clit, while his dick rubs against the spot I need.

Speeding up the pace, I feel myself rising higher and higher. I don't want this to end. I want to do this all night. "I—" I moan. "I—fuck." I sink down as far as I can into both of them and my orgasm rips me to shreds. My whole body convulses. My pussy and clit are almost too sensitive to be touched, but the boys don't let up. They pound into me and I think my body might split in half.

They ride out my orgasm with me until they both release themselves.

Zane drapes himself across my back and I lie down flat on Isaac's chest. We're all panting and trying to catch our breath. The air around us smells sweet and is hot enough to qualify my room as a sauna.

# Chapter 31

The room still smells like warmth and skin and something fragile I don't have a name for yet.

I can't remember the last time I felt this good.

I'm wrapped in the quiet aftermath, sitting cross-legged on the edge of the couch with a blanket pulled loosely around my shoulders. My pulse hasn't quite remembered how to slow down. Every nerve feels awake, humming like it's waiting for another touch—even though I'm already touched out in the best possible way.

Zane is sprawled on the floor at my feet, one arm thrown dramatically over his eyes like he's survived some great ordeal. "Well," he says, voice lazy and satisfied, "I think that officially qualifies as a team-building exercise."

I let out a surprised laugh, the sound breaking something open in my chest. "You're unbelievable."

"Thank you," he replies solemnly. "I work very hard at that."

Isaac doesn't laugh—but the corner of his mouth lifts, just barely. He's standing near the window, shirt still unbuttoned, the city lights painting him in soft gold and shadow. One hand rests on the back of the chair I was sitting in earlier, knuckles white like he hasn't fully come back to himself yet.

His eyes keep finding me—not in the sharp, assessing way they usually do. This is different. Unguarded. Almost reverent.

It makes my stomach flip.

Zane peeks at him through his fingers. "You're staring," he says. "Again. You're going to scare her."

"I'm not scared," I say softly.

Isaac's gaze snaps to mine at that, something dark and intense passing through his expression before he reins it in. He clears his throat. "You okay?"

The question is simple, but it lands heavy. Like he actually needs to know. I nod. "Yeah. I'm...yeah."

I don't have better words than that. Everything feels too big, too bright. Like I stepped into something I didn't know I was missing and now I can't imagine not standing in it.

Zane rolls onto his side and props himself up on one elbow, studying me with a thoughtful look that doesn't match his usual bravado. "You sure?" he asks, quieter now. "Because we can pretend none of that happened. Or we can pretend it only half happened. I'm very flexible with denial."

I smile, warmth blooming behind my ribs. "I don't want to pretend. I don't want to forget what happened between us."

Something shifts between them at that.

Isaac exhales slowly, like he's been holding his breath for longer than he realized. He crosses the room in two measured steps and stops in front of me. He doesn't touch me right away—just waits, giving me space, like he's afraid of doing the wrong thing.

The care in it nearly undoes me.

When he finally does reach out, it's just his knuckles brushing my knee. A question. An anchor.

Zane watches us for a beat, then grins. "Wow. Okay. So, this is happening. Great. Fantastic. I'm emotionally unprepared, but we'll power through."

I laugh again, softer this time, and Zane pushes himself to his feet. He leans down and presses a quick kiss to my temple—warm, affectionate, unguarded. "You're pretty incredible," he says, like it's a fact he's only just discovered. Then, quieter, to Isaac: "Don't make it weird."

Isaac huffs out something that might be a laugh. "You already did."

Zane throws his hands up. "I try."

The room settles into a strange, fragile calm. Not awkward, not tense. Just...new.

I've never been looked at like this before—like I matter in more than one way at once. Like I'm not a complication, but something precious they didn't expect and don't quite know what to do with yet. It's dizzying.

I pull the blanket tighter around myself, heart still racing, and stare out at the city beyond the glass. For a moment, it almost feels like the world has paused—like we're suspended in something soft and impossible.

# Chapter 32

At 11:47 p.m., the room seems to inhale and I find myself very close to falling asleep. The combination of adrenaline, fear, and pleasure have my limbs feeling useless.

The low hum of the scanner shifts—subtle, almost imperceptible—but Isaac catches it immediately. His spine straightens, shoulders locking into place like a weapon being armed. The air around him changes, the calm snapping into something sharp and alert.

A single, soft beep cuts through the apartment.

Not loud, not dramatic, but final.

Isaac doesn't look away from the screen. "Something isn't right."

Zane is already moving, eyes tracking the monitor as new data scrolls into place—pings, triangulations, red markers lighting up like a constellation. Whatever levity he was carrying earlier vanishes, replaced with cold focus.

"Signal spike," Zane mutters. "Multiple sources. They know someone is still watching them." His jaw tightens.

My stomach drops as I make my way between them to see what's going on with my own eyes.

Across the street, the office building reacts like it's been waiting for a cue. Lights shut off in jagged clusters—too fast, too uneven to be routine. Windows go dark, then blink back on in different patterns. Someone inside knows they've been burned.

Isaac reaches into the inside pocket of his jacket and pulls out a small device, thumb already pressing down. His voice is clipped, all command.

"Move. Now."

Whatever response comes back makes his jaw flex, but he doesn't relax.

In the street below, a figure appears at the front entrance of the building—head down, coat collar pulled high. He doesn't hesitate. Doesn't look around. He checks his phone once, then slips into a waiting car that rolls away without headlights.

Zane watches the windows long after the car is gone. "They're not retreating," he says quietly. "They're repositioning."

Isaac doesn't argue. He keeps counting. Seconds stretch into minutes. His gaze never leaves the door, like he's daring something to happen.

Nothing does.

Finally, he exhales through his nose. "That was the warning."

He powers down the scanner, movements efficient but tense. Zane shoulders his bag, glancing around the apartment like he's committing it to memory—or maybe regretting that it ever became part of this.

They hesitate. Both of them.

And the realization hits me harder than it should: I don't want them to leave. Not now. Not when the quiet feels this brittle.

Zane breaks the silence first. "We're going to have to follow them," he says, lighter than the moment deserves. "I'm sorry...and for the whole...breaking-into-your-home-on-a-holiday thing."

I huff softly. "You really know how to charm a girl."

He smiles, but it doesn't quite reach his eyes.

Isaac steps closer, stopping just short of my space. He studies my face like I'm a problem he hasn't solved yet—and maybe he doesn't like the variables.

"You're safe," he says. "Whatever comes next—it won't touch you."

I search his face, needing to believe him. "You're sure?"

Zane walks closer to me, wrapping his arm around my waist and pulling me closer to him. "Yes."

"We're sure," Isaac adds. Immediate. Absolute. No hesitation. "Both of us would do anything to keep you safe. And right now, we need to apprehend these fuckers to make sure they don't retaliate against your building. That would be our fault, and I wouldn't be able to live with myself."

"Tonight was everything with you." Zane punctuates this sentence with a sad smile.

Maybe they're as heartbroken about the night ending as I am.

Isaac places his palm against my cheek, and I lean into the warmth of his hand. This night has been more terrifying than I ever could've imagined. Even before all of this was happening, part of me was dreading another holiday without someone to keep me company. And somehow the universe answered with not just one man, but *two* men. Maybe I'm not as difficult to love as I've always convinced myself. Maybe this was one way to let me know that I'm ready to open my heart again. That you can find love in the strangest situations.

I'm equally split between feeling giddy over this realization and feeling like I could burst into tears at the thought that these two men I've spent all evening with, had *sex* with, will just disappear into the night to finish their job and I'll never see them again.

Then—

The deadbolt on my front door *screams*.

Metal shrieks as it's forced inward, the frame splintering with a violent crack that reverberates through the apartment.

The door buckles.

And the night finally explodes.

# Chapter 33

Isaac moves first. "Rose—"

Three men flood the entryway—dark jackets, gloved hands, faces half-hidden beneath hoods and intent. One of them already has a gun raised. His arm is steady and his eyes are cold. Another barrels forward like he's been waiting all night for permission to hurt someone.

The apartment erupts.

Isaac slams into the nearest man without hesitation, all controlled violence and momentum, driving him backward into the wall hard enough to rattle the frames. The impact makes my teeth clack together. Zane dives for cover, already moving, already reaching into his bag and coming up with his weapon in one smooth, practiced motion. Muscle memory.

I don't scream. There isn't time.

Adrenaline floods my system, sharp and clarifying, and my body moves before my fear can catch up. The second man lunges in my direction. I grab the empty wine bottle that was discarded on my coffee table earlier in the night—the one Zane picked on me about earlier.

It's heavy in my hand. Solid. Perfect. I step into the swing, just like Zane had joked about earlier and bring it down across his skull, aiming for the temple.

The sound is sickening—glass shattering, bone ringing. He crumples instantly, unconscious before he hits the floor.

For half a second, everything freezes.

The intruders stare in horror at their fallen partner. Zane and Isaac go still, too, shock flashing across their faces—not fear, but something close to awe. Maybe even relief that the violence hasn't been aimed at them earlier tonight.

Then the moment snaps.

The third man grabs my arm, yanking me backward hard enough to steal the breath from my lungs. I twist on instinct, driving my heel down onto his foot with everything I have. I feel something give way beneath my shoe. He howls.

Isaac is there a heartbeat later.

He rips the man away from me and slams him into the doorframe with brutal precision. Zane disarms the gunman in a blur—wrist twisted, weapon clattering to the floor. A sharp crack. A grunt. Another body goes down.

Zane disarms the gunman with brutal efficiency. Another sharp crack, a grunt. Another body hits the floor.

And then—

Silence.

Three men. One unconscious. Two groaning, painfully aware that this has not gone the way they planned.

Zane swears under his breath, running a hand through his hair.

Isaac drags one of the conscious men upright, pins him against the wall. His jaw tightens, something dark and controlled passing behind his eyes. He knocks the man out cold and lets him drop like dead weight.

My breathing is heavy and loud. My chest rises and falls with the effort of catching my breath.

The apartment is wrecked—broken glass crunching underfoot, wine soaking into the rug, the air sharp with adrenaline gone sour. My hands start to shake now that there's room for it.

Zane exhales first, slow and deliberate. "Well, that answers that."

Isaac scans the room again, methodical as ever. Door. Windows. Bodies. Shattered frame. His blue eyes don't linger on me—not like they did before. Whatever calculation he's running now, I'm no longer part of it. No longer a major cause of concern.

"They tracked the signal," Zane says quietly, his voice low and stripped of humor as he surveys the wreckage of my apartment one last time.

Isaac nods once, sharp and decisive. "Yeah. No shit."

There's a beat—heavy, deliberate—where neither of them looks at me. Zane exhales through his nose, then straightens, all resolve and purpose snapping back into place.

"This is where we step out," he says. "We'll dispose of them. Clean it up. Make sure there's no trail."

And just like that, it's over.

Or at least...*we* are.

The shift is subtle but unmistakable. The charged air from earlier drains away, replaced by something colder, cleaner, professional. Isaac is already shrugging into his jacket, movements efficient, mind clearly miles ahead of this moment.

"You stay here," he says, tone firm but not unkind. "Lock the door behind us."

I nod automatically, the motion instinctive. Obedient. But something inside my chest sinks anyway, settling heavy and hollow.

They're all business again—focused, contained, untouchable. Whatever electric, fragile thing that existed between us earlier had evaporated, leaving distance in its wake. The apartment suddenly feels too large, too quiet. I wrap my arms around myself, fingers digging into my sleeves as if I can hold onto the warmth they're already taking with them.

Used, whispers a cruel little voice I don't want to listen to, as my eyes well with tears. I will the tears to disappear before they see how emotional I am.

Forgotten.

*Again.*

Zane must see it on my face, because he slows near the door. Isaac does, too, pausing mid-step like something's finally clicked. He turns back toward me, his expression softening in a way that catches me off guard. Forgetting the discarded bodies that are littered throughout my apartment.

"Hey," Isaac says gently. "This isn't us leaving you."

Zane nods in agreement, his usual edge dulled. "We're absolutely not leaving you alone right now. We need to make sure you're safe."

The word *safe* lands differently now—heavier, more personal. Zane steps closer, voice dropping, grounding. "We'll take shifts staying with you tonight while the other one cleans up this mess."

My throat tightens. I hate how much I need to hear it. "You will?" I ask, hating how small and hopeful it sounds.

Isaac's mouth curves faintly, something warm flickering in his eyes. "And then in the morning, we'll take you to brunch."

That does it.

I blink, emotion catching me off guard. "I love brunch."

Zane's smile lights up his entire face, a hint of that familiar charm slipping back into place. "Then it's settled. Valentine's Day is canceled forevermore." He folds one arm in front of his stomach and the other behind his back before offering a bow.

My inner child beams at his comment, his statement confirming that she has finally found her support for canceling Valentine's Day. Though this is one day she'll definitely never forget.

"Tomorrow," Isaac adds smoothly. "The fifteenth will be our new holiday for the three of us."

I huff out a weak laugh, shaking my head. I thought I felt disbelief earlier when both of these men finally gave into their desires. I'm still stunned that what they both wanted was...me. "So, what—you're saying I have two boyfriends now?"

They exchange a glance—brief, loaded, almost amused. Isaac shrugs, easy and sincere. "If that's what you want."

Zane tilts his head, lips twitching. "Let's not rush it. You need to take me out to dinner first before I agree to a relationship."

I laugh for real this time, the sound loosening something tight and aching in my chest.

They lean in one after the other, pressing gentle kisses to my cheeks—warm, grounding, unhurried. Reassurance without expectation. Promises without pressure. They close their hands around mine and hang on even after they've started to walk away.

"Isaac will stay with you now," Zane says. "Try to get some rest."

Then he's gone, dragging an unconscious body behind him, and the door closes softly.

Isaac wraps his arms around my shoulders and presses me into his warm chest. I've never felt so *safe* before in my entire life.

It's the first time I realize that I never really wanted to be alone tonight. The thought that that was how I was going to spend my night makes me sad. I already miss Zane's playfulness, but I'm safe in Isaac's arms.

He scoops me up without effort, one arm under my knees, the other firm at my back. I let out a soft laugh, fingers curling into his shirt as he carries me down the hall, each step unhurried, careful. Isaac lowers me onto the bed like it's exactly where I belong before crawling in next to me.

And in that moment, I do something I didn't think I'd do this evening, I smile to myself feeling genuinely happy.

This doesn't feel like an ending.

It feels like a promise that maybe Valentine's Day isn't so bad after all.

# Acknowledgments

To Alyx, Amanda, and Zoe, this novella would have some terrible title and poorly named characters if it weren't for you three. Thank you for being some of my biggest fans—I'm grateful to do life with you.

To my husband and my son, I apologize once again for not being able to dedicate this one to you. It's even spicier. Though, Daniel, the way you make me laugh inspired some of the banter in this story. There will always be a little piece of you in my dream-boat male main characters. Maybe one day I'll write something that's not so smutty? OWEN, YOU SHOULDN'T BE READING THIS!

To Emily, my forever first beta reader of all things. You make me feel like I can do absolutely anything.

To my ride-or-die editor, Vicky, I will follow you wherever you go, even into the depths of hell. Thank you for, once again, working your magic on my manuscript, even when I said "Hey, I have a novella releasing in less than two months!"

Always to you, my beautiful reader, whether this is your first read by me or you loved *Beneath Your Lies* enough to keep coming back. You are why I get to do what I love.

I always try to sneak sentimental pieces into my story, and for anyone who has ever felt unlovable or like you are "too much", you are so worthy of love and you could be more. Always be more. I love you.

# About the author

Nicole J. Owens is the author of *Beneath Your Lies*. She currently resides in Charlotte, NC with her husband, their three-year-old son, and two dogs, Benny the Bernedoodle and Ruby the Miniature Cockapoo. *Taken by Surprise* is her second published book.

www.nicolejowens.com

Instagram: @AuthorNicoleJOwens

TikTok: @AuthorNicoleJOwens

Threads: @AuthorNicoleJOwens

Facebook.com/AuthorNicoleJOwens